He visually worshiped her every feature. "I'm still not."

His kiss was everything Marlayna remembered—and more. She gave up trying to think and let herself be swept away by the sheer sorcery of his touch. His tongue gently trespassed into the inviting depths of her mouth, savoring the honeyed sweetness.

With a low moan, Marlayna pulled her mouth free and brushed away her tears and then his with gentle fingertips. "I'm not sure why I'm kissing you, Noah Drake."

"Because you still love me."

"That's not good enough."

ELAINE RACO CHASE

recently exchanged Schenectady, New York, for the sunny beaches of east coast Florida. Here, with her husband, daughter, and son, she enjoys swimming, teaches creative writing, and reads detective novels. Formerly an advertising copywriter, Elaine writes romantic comedies and believes loving and laughing make wonderful bedfellows.

Dear Reader:

SILHOUETTE DESIRE is an exciting new line of contemporary romances from Silhouette Books. During the past year, many Silhouette readers have written in telling us what other types of stories they'd like to read from Silhouette, and we've kept these comments and suggestions in mind in developing SILHOUETTE DESIRE.

DESIREs feature all of the elements you like to see in a romance, plus a more sensual, provocative story. So if you want to experience all the excitement, passion and joy of falling in love, then SILHOUETTE DESIRE is for you.

Karen Solem
Editor-in-Chief
Silhouette Books

ELAINE RACO CHASE
Lady Be Bad

Silhouette Desire

Published by Silhouette Books New York

America's Publisher of Contemporary Romance

Silhouette Books by Elaine Raco Chase

Calculated Risk (DES #104)
Lady Be Bad (DES #138)

 SILHOUETTE BOOKS, a Division of Simon & Schuster, Inc.
1230 Avenue of the Americas, New York, N.Y. 10020

Distributed by Pocket Books

ISBN: 0-671-46228-8

First Silhouette Books printing May, 1984

10 9 8 7 6 5 4 3 2 1

America's Publisher of Contemporary Romance

Printed in the U.S.A.

BC91

I would like to express my thanks to the following people for their help in researching this book:

Warren C. Chase, Waterbury, Vermont, for pamphlets, brochures and navigational charts on Jorstadt and the Thousand Islands;

Marion Smith Collins, Calhoun, Georgia, for her knowledge on the Atlanta area;

Mary Gaspary, City Island Library, Daytona Beach, Florida, for her never-ending search for information on all fronts;

Wendy Zemball, C.S.T. R.N., Ormond Beach, Florida, for her technical and medical skills.

The greatest joy in my life has been becoming acquainted with my agent, Denise Marcil, and a very special group of talented romance authors who never fail to surround me with love, inspiration and laughter: Anne, Barbara, Dixie, Jayne and Suzanne. Single-handedly we all keep AT&T smiling over profits.

1

A new record! Five pieces of mail in two weeks! I restocked the fridge and left a dozen cheese Danish. Mr. Wingate and Miss Davies called to say they'd be over later. Congratulations too on what's underneath!

Pearl

Marlayna O'Brian smiled at her housekeeper's exuberantly scrawled message. The curve on her lips turned wistful. Five pieces of mail in two weeks, and that was after living and working in Manhattan for nearly six years. It seemed that her initial goal of becoming lost in a city of seven million had been reached.

Sliding the yellow legal-sized paper to one side, Marlayna viewed the cover of *Vogue* that had been so carefully shielded and saw herself. "The lost has been discovered!"

One professionally sculptured eyebrow raised slightly, almost mockingly, as she studied the full-face shot. Cool blue gray eyes stared at a pair of more cosmetically enhanced duplicates, traveled upward to the sophisticated sable curls that frothed a high forehead before focusing on the coral-tinted Mona Lisa smile that the photographer had coaxed.

The woman in the photo looked mysterious, provocative and earthy—nothing more than a slick, colorful, glossy lie. "I'm sure they're all thrilled." Marlayna played with the zipper on the navy jacket of her jogging suit before tossing the fashion magazine back on the glass foyer table. Her white sneakers maneuvered an oversized nylon travel bag soccer-style into the quiet apartment while she examined the remaining four envelopes.

Con Edison's computer-printed power bill requested a hefty amount for keeping her cool during the thirty-one hot and humid days of July; Bell Telephone was billing her for the usual monthly minimum—no extra charges for long distance or information calls; and American Express asked that she not leave home without sending them their allotment. The last piece of mail seemed to demand to be opened by something a bit more elegant than her marauding, albeit perfectly manicured, thumbnail.

Marlayna high-stepped over her luggage and skipped across the delicately patterned Oriental carpet, around the cream sofa to the petite oak lady's desk in the alcove. Centered on the leather blotter was an ivory-handled letter opener. She gave an irreverent grin as her fingers smoothed the rich parchment envelope and outlined the raised *K* embedded in the black wax that sealed the silver-banded flap.

The telephone's shrill interruption made Marlayna's precise slice go jaggedly awry. "Yes?"

"How was your flight back?"

She smiled as Paul Wingate's lazy voice reached her ear. "Nicely cool, unlike my assignment." With her hip balanced on the edge of the desk, she slowly extracted an engraved card while she continued to talk. "Honestly, Paul, why is it always the fur company who decides to have their winter coats photographed in the Mojave Desert in the dead of summer?"

His laughter was rich. "You should know by now that fashion is an ass-backward industry, kiddo." Paul turned serious. "I hope the dry heat didn't ruin the 'Face of the Century.'"

Now it was Marlayna's turn to laugh. "Strange"— her fingers skidded across her makeup-free complexion—"I've had this same face for twenty-nine years and no one has ever thought it worthy of this much concern."

"Don't let Arthur Kingman hear you slander your pores," Paul answered. "Since you've been 'The Face of Kingman Cosmetics,' sales have tripled, King Arthur's been a pussycat to deal with, and my migraines have disappeared. You're hot stuff these days, and Kingman's anxious to make sure your face belongs only to him. You should have seen his expression when he saw the newest layout; the man ran out of adjectives. Listen, kiddo, I have big plans for you. . . ."

But Marlayna wasn't listening. She wasn't feeling. She wasn't even breathing. She just continued to stare at the embossed invitation, completely hypnotized by what she was reading:

Arthur Kingman cordially invites you to a dual celebration—the engagement of his daughter Gwen Lynn to Noah Drake and the opening of Kingman Castle, Jorstadt Island, in the St. Lawrence.

Arthur Kingman and Noah Drake. The two names ballooned to skyscraper proportions. The first man was part of her present, the second was part of her past and the masculine voice in her ear was droning on and on with plans for her future.

"P—P—Paul . . ." Marlayna stuttered, then took a deep breath before continuing, "Paul, what is the status of my contract with Kingman Cosmetics?"

"I just got through telling you he approved the final layout," came Paul's grousing reminder. "Kingman's doubled his offer for you for another year, but I've been approached by another cosmetic company. They want you for a 'switch' campaign and—"

"Sign with the competition, Paul," she directed in a terse voice. "I don't think King Arthur will ever want to see this face again once he finds me in bed with his daughter's fiancé."

Marlayna hung up the receiver, effectively terminating Paul Wingate's horrified shout.

"Hello, Paul. What took you so long?" Marlayna quipped, giving a cursory inspection and a consoling pat to the apartment door that had just taken a rather brutal pounding.

"Sleeping Beauty." Paul jerked his thumb back over his shoulder at the yawning woman who slowly followed in his anxious wake.

"Hi, sweetie." Sylvia Davies greeted her friend with her usual hug and kiss. The kiss, however, turned into

10

another yawn. "Am I all together?" Brown eyes blinked owlishly at Marlayna and waited for approval.

"I've never seen you untogether in the six years I've known you."

"Can you believe the nerve of this guy, pounding on my door and waking me up at this ghastly hour?" Sylvia paused to check herself in the brass-framed entry mirror.

Paul looked in disgust at her, then at his trembling hands. "It's four o'clock on Sunday afternoon, Sylvia." His hands were first shoved into the pockets of his thin denim jacket and then into his jeans. "That's hardly a ghastly hour."

She continued to study her reflection, refastening a stray wisp of platinum hair that had escaped her elegant chignon and using her pinky to neaten the corners of a mauve sculpted mouth. "Paulie, you know I use Sunday to recover from Friday and Saturday and get invigorated for work on Monday."

Sylvia turned to face him, crossing her arms over the front of her ivory silk jumpsuit. "Besides, what is all the fuss? It's done me a world of good to hear that this lady is finally going bad. What we have in Marlayna is a woman who has teased and charmed her way out of any and every potentially intimate situation. The lady who always says no is finally saying yes.

"Although, pet"—she shifted her gaze to her smiling female companion—"don't you think you should wait and see little Gwen's fiancé? I mean, King Art's baby princess is only twenty-three, and perhaps the burgeoning little prince is the same. Could it be that younger men are your downfall?" Her left eyebrow raised, making three unaccustomed wrinkles on her smooth forehead. "Or is this a ploy to make Arthur

11

jealous? Everyone in the industry knows he begins to harden and salivate just looking at your photos."

Paul shook a clenched fist in warning. "Marlayna, if you're trying to make Kingman jealous, use somebody else. Gwen is his second greatest treasure after his cosmetic empire."

Sylvia nodded. "I hate to admit this, but I agree with Paulie." Her fingers combed back a lock of silver hair that had fallen across his eyebrow. "In fact, I'd even suggest you use Paulie, but then everyone knows that he'd only get excited if your name was Marlon."

"Now, now, that's enough, you two." Marlayna quickly stepped between her two ready-to-spar friends. "Come on inside and we can talk. I've made coffee and Pearl left some Danish."

"I doubt if coffee will neutralize Sylvia's acid tongue," Paul returned sarcastically.

"Nothing will do that, pet," Sylvia purred, "but I need at least three cups of hot caffeine before I hear one more word of this story."

"At least calm my nerves about one thing," Paul persisted, dropping onto a cream sofa cushion. "Are you doing this to make Kingman jealous?"

Marlayna settled sideways in a mauve swivel rocker and gestured at the oak cocktail table for them to help themselves to coffee and pastries. "You both know Arthur Kingman has approached me on too many occasions. But the man's not looking for a real woman. Arthur wants a centerpiece, an ornament; he wants a perfect model for a wife." Her lips curved and her eyes flashed with impish delight. "We all know I'm none of the above."

Waving away the steaming cup Sylvia was offering, Paul reached for the crystal decanter next to the silver coffeepot and filled another delicate china cup with brandy. She was right, he mused in thoughtful silence, Marlayna O'Brian was neither a centerpiece, an ornament nor a model.

He and Sylvia had turned her into the latter. Marlayna was a woman with two stage mothers, although he preferred to be labeled Pygmalion to her Galatea. Paul took a healthy swallow of brandy and thought about all the Galateas he had sculpted in his twenty-five years as head of the international corps of Wingate models.

There were too many to count. Paul was a beauty peddler, dipping into a seemingly endless supply of comely talent. Some models had gone on to become actors and actresses; some had become personalities; a few had even become authors. He had polished and promoted all his protégés and earned millions in the process. None of them, however, had moved into his personal life, into his very soul the way Marlayna O'Brian had over the years.

She was nothing if not solid, unpretentious and— Paul gave an inward chuckle—still disgustingly wholesome. That was the reason she was in great demand. A face that looked virginal on a curvy, womanly body. Marlayna hadn't wanted to be a model, hadn't come to the Big Apple seeking the glossy page, but she had handled the whole nutty, narcissistic industry with panache.

His blue gaze studied the smiling woman who was playfully half-rocking, half-swiveling in the chair. Marlayna looked happy. An expression Paul knew had been an elusive one for the last six years. His hand shook slightly as he raised the liquor-filled cup to his mouth. Six years! Another gulp of brandy instantly seared him from the inside out in fiery, delicious heat.

Eyes closed, his silver head lolling back against the

cushion, Paul let that mellowed warmth transport him back six years—to the first time he had ever seen Marlayna O'Brian. On the way to check on final arrangements for a fashion show with the buyer at Lord & Taylor's, he had cut through the cosmetic department. There he encountered Sylvia Davies beginning to work her magic on one of the most pale, depressed, pinched faces he had ever seen.

He had mouthed "good luck" to Sylvia behind the young woman's back and continued on his way. An hour later, on the way out of the department store, he saw the finished face—a face that had come alive under skilled hands and color-filled makeup pots. And Paul Wingate knew that if a face could hold his rapt attention, it could hold a client's.

"So the ugly duckling was really a swan after all," came his firm pronouncement. He watched the woman's artfully shadowed blue gray eyes shift toward Sylvia in wary silence. "Tell her I'm famous but quite harmless."

"He's famous but very, very harmless," the platinum blonde dutifully recited. "And she was always a swan, Paul," Sylvia plumped out the younger woman's dark curls. "I'm just helping her out of hibernation. Marlayna O'Brian meet Paul Wingate, Wingate Modeling Agency. Marlayna's staying with me for a while."

"You with a female roomie, Sylvia?" Paul's eyebrows raised. "I'm surprised Manhattan's still standing."

"Add caustic to the list of Paulie's attributes," Lord & Taylor's head cosmetic buyer directed to her wide-eyed friend.

"Caustic but charming," he added, then aimed a

full blast of charm toward her companion. "Have you ever thought of becoming a model?"

"I'm a lab technician at the Raydon Medical Laboratory."

His ear found her languid accent soothing. "And not from New York?"

"Atlanta," Marlayna supplied. "I've been here just six weeks."

"How about discussing your new career over a cup of coffee?" Paul invited.

"My . . . my . . . new career?" she stammered. "I'm sorry, Mr. Wingate, but you've made a mistake. Models are thin and beautiful and I'm not . . ."

His hand slid under her elbow. "Coffee, no sugar or cream." He guided her off the stool and continued to overrule her every stuttered objection. "You're the perfect height, maybe a little too busty and hippy, but then again with that curvy figure and the ebony hair you'll stand out over the batch of California sun-toasted blondes that cavort on the fashion pages."

Over black coffee for him and a glass of water for her, Paul used all of his persuasive powers, threw in monetary enticements and an overflow of other glamorous seducements—all to no avail.

"I'm really sorry, Mr. Wingate," she repeated for the millionth time. "I'm not interested. Thank you for your time and trouble and the water and the crackers."

"I'm not giving up," Paul warned, sliding a card into the pocket of her white lab coat as she stood to leave. "Sylvia should have also added *pest* to my character sketch. When I see something I want, I go after it until I get it."

Paul had kept his promise, and with Sylvia's help,

he became an almost weekly intruder into Marlayna O'Brian's life. But the lady was adamant and insistent, and after a month, he did give up. Five weeks later, she came knocking on the door of his plush upper East Side skyscraper office. Her face was paler and more pinched than the first time he had seen her, her mental condition more depressed, and her body, thinner and fragile looking.

"Mr. Wingate, I . . . I lost my lab job and I've got a lot of medical bills. If you still think you'd like to take on the job of making me into a model. . . ."

He had stared for a long moment into bleak gray blue eyes. "I think I'm going to take on the job of making you a happy, healthy woman first. What has Sylvia been doing with you?"

"Just taking care of me," Marlayna whispered. "If it wasn't for her. . . ."

"What happened?"

"Divorce and a . . . a miscarriage."

Paul's hands cradled her face. "That's all in the past, Marlayna. With Sylvia and me for friends, you're going to have a wonderful present and future."

It took nearly a year to get Marlayna mentally and physically healthy. The more Paul became involved with her, the more beautiful she became—a beauty that had nothing to do with her face and figure. She was intelligent, compassionate, witty and a natural confidante. Her low-key manner was engaging, and when she spoke, he found he wanted to hear her every word, straining so as not to miss a thing she said.

He had taken the business side of Marlayna O'Brian slowly. Her initiation was the photo portfolio. As Paul had anticipated, the camera loved her and seemingly from any angle. Her complexion now at twenty-nine still held the youthful freshness it had at twenty-three, her facial bone structure was soft but strong, and thick, curly, nearly black hair enhanced Marlayna's features.

She was five foot eight, beautifully proportioned and, even though she was ten pounds over what the agency normally would allow, the weight looked perfect on her, making her more realistic to the millions of women who read fashion magazines and buy beauty products.

Over the ensuing years, Paul had brought Marlayna gently through the ranks: fashion shows, catalogue work, various magazine layouts; her face was just now debuting on the leading magazine covers. Last year she had been featured in the fabled *Sports Illustrated* bathing suit issue. Then had come Arthur Kingman's excited phone call and an exclusive, six-figure-a-year contract to be "The Face of Kingman Cosmetics."

Kingman Cosmetics! Paul snapped to attention, drained the last of the brandy and growled, "Christ, Sylvia, how much coffee do you need!"

Sylvia's hand stopped halfway toward the silver pot. "Pour yourself another brandy, pet, and take a cue from our hostess and relax." Her amber brown gaze shifted to Marlayna. "You are very relaxed, aren't you."

"Disgustingly so," she laughingly agreed. "I feel wonderful."

"Sometimes anticipating sex is better than the actual event," her friend cautioned with rueful wisdom.

"Not in this case," came Marlayna's smug rejoinder.

Sylvia reached for the engraved card propped against a blue Chinese vase on the end table. "Noah Drake. Hmmmm . . ." She repeated the name half a dozen times. "I like the way it just rolls off one's tongue." Smiling, she added: "It does sound too virile a name for little Gwen to handle."

"Please . . ." Paul turned the word into a groan.

"Now, now, Paulie," Sylvia retorted matter-of-factly, "perhaps if your mother had named you . . . um . . . Derek . . . you would vacation in Aspen instead of Fire Island." She shifted her attention back to the card. "I wonder what a Noah Drake looks like?"

Marlayna didn't even have to close her eyes to remember. "He's six feet tall, has dark brown hair and chocolate eyes. A nice face, not hard or forbidding. A ready smile, a beard that needs to be shaved twice a day and"—she favored them with a wink and a grin—"two moles—one on his left earlobe and one on the inside of his right thigh."

Paul and Sylvia traded speculative glances. "He's a photographer," the silver-haired agent accused, but Marlayna shook her head no. "A male model, then?" Again the silent negative answer was repeated.

"Drake . . . Drake . . . Drake," Sylvia chanted the last name. "I know that name. I've heard it before."

"Society column?" Paul pressed. "Gossip? Ad agency? Buyer? Designer?"

"Paulie!" she screeched. "Have another drink and shut up for a minute, would you." Sylvia massaged her temples with gentle fingertips and strove to concentrate. The name Drake rang a bell, but the sound was distant and muffled. Through half-closed eyes she watched Marlayna enjoy a second cheese Danish.

The longer she focused on Marlayna, the louder and clearer the bell was sounding. Airplane! Another image burst into Sylvia's mind. Her eyes widened then shut tight. Airplanes had become one of her standard modes of transportation. As head cosmetics buyer for

Lord & Taylor, Sylvia jetted across the continents buying new products and training new store personnel.

A reminiscent smile curved her lips and softened a face that was seldom ruffled by any expression that might possibly leave a visible trace. It was on a plane, returning to Manhattan from a training assignment in Atlanta, that Sylvia had ended up with a most unusual souvenir—the ebony-haired woman now seated in the mauve rocker.

Marlayna hadn't been so casually sprawled in the airplane seat, Sylvia recalled. She had strapped herself in much too tightly, three air-sick bags were within easy reach, both air blowers were aimed full blast in her face, while her death-grip left prints in the metal chair arms.

Sylvia reluctantly belted herself into the seat next to this mass of nerves. "First flight?"

After a cough, a throat clearing and a hiccup, Marlayna had finally managed a weak "Yes."

"How about a drink, sweetie?"

"Do you think it will help?"

"It'll help me," she quipped. Sylvia had, for some unexplained reason, taken an immediate interest in her seatmate. She usually just slept on planes, unless of course her seatmate was an attractive man, but this time Sylvia found herself making the overtures, seeking answers to why blue gray eyes looked so soulful, why such a young face looked so tired and troubled, why this child-woman was heading to a city that could gobble up and spit you out with no apologies whatsoever.

"This is what's so lovely about flying first class." She clicked her ice-filled glass with Marlayna's. "A couple of these before takeoff and you're not even aware that you've entered the wild blue yonder." Sylvia dipped into her cocktail-party-chatter reserve and babbled effusively about absolutely nothing. The ploy was effective enough so that her companion had not even given a second thought to the fact they were now at thirty-five thousand feet.

"So tell me"—she changed tactics as they sipped their third gin and tonic—"are you another dancer or actress aiming to strut your stuff across a Broadway stage and make all the critics take notice?"

Marlayna shook her head. "I am . . . I was a lab technician at Grady Memorial Hospital."

"Oh, and now you're going to look through a microscope in Manhattan?"

"I . . . I hadn't really thought about that."

Sylvia's confused expression was a duplicate of her companion's. "Sweetie, just why are you on this plane?"

Marlayna took two more swallows of gin. "I . . . I'm running away." Tears flowed, and Sylvia found herself becoming privy to the most unusual story.

"Now let me see if I've got this all straight, pet." She handed Marlayna the last flowered tissue in her purse-pack. "You were quite happily married for two years, renting this cute two-bedroom World War II bungalow . . ."

"All brick with a fireplace, near Georgia Tech."

"Right . . ." She humored her. "You worked days as an emergency room admissions clerk and went to school nights to become a lab technician. He was a construction foreman days and was working on a degree nights."

"He had to take only three more credits and his final exam before he became an architect. He even had an agency offer him a job!"

Sylvia managed a benign smile. "Then last month you cut some grocery coupons out of the sports section, he got mad, you wouldn't kiss him before he went to work, there was an accident, he was badly hurt, he still won't see or talk to you and now wants a divorce."

Marlayna nodded and sniffed. "That's it. That's the whole thing. It's so simple and confusing and stupid."

"Sounds like the stuff most men are made of, pet."

"I just don't understand any of it," Marlayna continued to babble. "He forbid the doctors and nurses to tell me a thing. The security guard threatened to haul me out of the intensive care waiting area if I didn't leave voluntarily. Then . . . this hateful lawyer showed up and started taking inventory of the house and asking me all sorts of . . . of horrible personal questions and . . . and I can't get any answers from anybody and . . . and . . . I just have no family to turn to . . . all our friends are as confused as I am . . . and . . . and I don't want a divorce. I love my husband."

"How old are you, sweetie?"

"Almost twenty-three."

"Well, I'm thirty-six and I've had my fill of husbands."

"You . . . you have?"

Sylvia nodded. "Three were three too many. Do you know my second husband divorced me because I didn't iron his shirts like his mother and my dumplings weren't flaky enough."

"That's pretty silly."

"Sillier than someone divorcing you over cutting coupons?" Sylvia signaled for another round of drinks. "Take a little advice from a scarred veteran of marital world wars one, two and three; if this bozo gets uptight over a few holes in the newspaper, you're well rid of him. I think it's pretty damn shabby for him to hit you with a fast-talking shyster lawyer. You didn't sign anything, did you?"

"Lots of things."

"Oh, God." She gave her a consoling pat. "Don't worry, pet, you have found a champion in Aunt Sylvia. I'll introduce you to my attorney. Hal is a genius at handling this type of thing. He does squeeze blood from a stone."

Marlayna bit her lip. "Is he . . . expensive?"

"Good things are always expensive."

"I don't have much money left. The plane fare was more than I thought because all they had was first class, and it'll take me some time to find a job and a place to live."

One perfectly manicured fingernail lightly scratched one perfectly blushed cheek. "I just happen to know the owner of an independent medical lab. We'll get you in there and"—Sylvia stared at her for a moment before coming to a decision—"and you can move into my apartment until you get bankrolled. I don't think you're in any condition to deal with the cunning worms that inhabit the Big Apple."

"I . . . I don't know. That's a very generous offer. I . . . you don't even know me. . . . I don't even know you . . . I . . ."

Sylvia watched the tears erupt again. "The first time I get to play the Good Samaritan and I get it kicked back into my face."

"Oh, no . . . I'm sorry . . . I didn't mean . . ."

"Sweetie, you don't plan to cry forever, do you? Listen, I'm perfectly harmless; you can check with my minister, my landlord, call my mother." She extended her hand. "I'm Sylvia Davies, head cosmetics buyer for the last three years for Lord & Taylor."

"I'm Marlayna D——," her voice faltered. "O'Brian. Marlayna O'Brian. That . . . that lawyer said my husband wanted his name back."

Sylvia made a rude noise. "And what is that bastard's name?"

"Noah . . . Noah Drake."

Noah Drake! The bell in Sylvia's head exploded. She lunged to her feet, stared at Marlayna and then turned to Paul Wingate. A mauve-tinted fingernail tapped the engraved invitation. "Noah Drake is her ex-husband!"

2

Marlayna's calm "That's right" made a distressed Sylvia sit down and a distraught Paul Wingate stand up.

"What do you mean 'that's right'?" he shouted. "After what you went through. What *he* put you through." His own face became bleak remembering her anguish. His hands began to gesture wildly. "How can you blithely sit there . . . say you actually crave that man . . . that you want him. . . ."

"Stop babbling, Paulie." Sylvia tugged the hem of his jacket. "Sit down and let's hear from her." She fixed a keen eye on Marlayna. "I think it's about time you did some talking and made sense of this whole situation."

"I suppose so." Suddenly, Marlayna's relaxed mood vanished. She pushed free of the rocker and aimlessly paced back and forth across the flower-strewn wool carpet. "When I first saw the name Noah

Drake printed on that invitation, I was thrilled, excited and blessedly relieved to find he was alive and apparently quite healthy."

"That was your *first* reaction," Sylvia countered: "What about your second?" she invited, reaching for more coffee.

Marlayna's full lips thinned in a tight smile. "My *second* reaction was more emotional." She stared in seemingly rapt fascination at her clenching and unclenching hands. "There was *my* husband linked with another woman." Unseeing eyes stared at her companions. "I wanted to kill both of them, slowly and quite brutally." She blinked rapidly, shook her head and gave a scared little laugh. "I found it interesting to see how little it took to turn a nice, civilized pacifist like myself into a kill-crazy savage."

"Women mourn while men replace," Sylvia sarcastically expounded the old maxim.

"I do not want to be replaced," Marlayna intoned with firm finality. "I do not intend to be replaced." Her bravado suddenly vanished. "My God." She dropped onto the edge of the coffee table. "To me Noah has been irreplaceable." Her eyes pooled with tears. "I know it sounds corny, but I took my wedding vows seriously. Till death do us part—for me there's been no other man, no love, no nothing during the past six years!"

Paul cleared his throat. "Nothing for you," he pointed out in a careful monotone, "but obviously your Noah Drake has——"

"I've got to see and hear *that* for myself."

"We've turned into a masochist, have we?" His response was cool.

"I'm not, it's just . . ."

"Just insane." Paul's anger grew. "My God, Marlayna, think back and remember how you were." His thumb and forefinger caught her chin, forcing her averted eyes to meet his challenging gaze. "I remember. I remember all too well what a complete mental, emotional and physical cripple you were. And all of it was due to Noah Drake." His fingers squeezed tighter. "Is that what you want for yourself again?"

"No, but . . ."

"Damn you!" His eyes blazed. "There shouldn't be any *but!* Look at how far you've come. Look at all you've done in the last half-dozen years without him. You don't need Noah Drake. What can he give you that you can't give yourself?"

His tone gentled; his fingers tenderly stroked her tear-damp cheeks and combed through her hair. "You've got it all: a fantastic apartment, a housekeeper, designer clothes, money, friends, a blooming career, you travel all over the world." Paul highlighted an impressive list. "What on earth are you lacking? Just what in hell can Noah Drake give you that you don't already have or can't buy?"

"Answers." Marlayna cried the word. "Noah is the man with all the answers. I want them. I deserve them." She pulled herself together. "I need to get them. I intend to get them!"

She was back on her feet. "Look, Paul, I know it's hard for you, but I . . . Sylvia, you must be able to understand . . . oh, damn." Marlayna's two feeble attempts at explaining herself failed miserably. She inhaled deeply and when she spoke again, her voice was steadier.

"All right, Paul, let's talk about all those material things you mentioned. This very elegant, East Side duplex, as you know, is a sublet from a woman in Brazil who still hasn't made the Internal Revenue

Service see it her way on five years' worth of tax returns. I'm just a visitor here, a guest with a three-times-a-week housekeeper who is part of the lease and makes sure I don't hurt anything. All the designer clothes? They're perks from some of the modeling jobs." She expanded the cuff on her fleece jogging jacket. "You can see how simple my tastes are. The other outfits just collect dust hanging in the bedroom closet."

The smile she offered Paul was almost a plea. "The career has been a happy accident. An accident that you've had more fun with than I have. The traveling goes with the job as does the money—money that you keep reminding me to spend but that I keep putting in the bank." Marlayna resumed her seat on the coffee table. Her right hand took Sylvia's; her left took Paul's. "You two are my only real friends. All the others are the usual supercilious, shallow hangers-on that come and go as quickly as a summer breeze. If all this"—her dark head nodded—"were to disappear, to end this very second, you two are the ones that I'd mourn."

It was Sylvia who finally ventured to speak, her tone quietly sympathetic. "You have been in mourning all these years, haven't you."

"Deep mourning." Marlayna nodded, squeezing both their hands before letting go. "If Noah had been killed, the mourning would have had an end. But a divorce—especially ours—left me with so many questions. Frustrations, actually, that have eaten away at my life."

Her blue gray eyes were bleak. "Since I read that invitation, my life suddenly became balanced. I'm anxious to see him, anxious to have all my questions answered. If it's true, if our marriage is really supposed to be over, I have to go back to it, confront the ghosts, solve the mystery. Then, I'll be able to go forward toward a new life."

Marlayna turned to Paul. "During the past years, I've forced you to pencil in my future. Now, once I see and talk to Noah, we can write me in ink. One way or another, Noah Drake is going to give me back my past. Then I'll be able to live and enjoy the present and dream about the future."

"Do you think it's wise to put all your eggs in Noah Drake's basket?" Paul countered. "He cracked them before."

Sylvia cleared her throat. "I hungered and chased after my first husband," she confessed, "and ultimately got George back from another woman." She gave Marlayna's knee a warning squeeze. "He was an even bigger disappointment the second time around."

"I've been thinking a lot about that, too." She sighed, wiping a weary hand over her face. "I wonder just how accurate my memories are. Have my dreams and longing blown Noah all out of proportion? Have I bestowed on him godlike qualities he never deserved?"

"He certainly doesn't deserve you," Paul said rudely. "I'm sorry, Marlayna, but it seems to me you've deliberately clung to the past and ignored everything else. I'm not sure you rate one speck of sympathy."

"She's not asking for sympathy, you clod," Sylvia snapped. "She's asking for us to understand." Her brown gaze shifted to her friend. "I, for one, understand perfectly and I should think with all the womanly hormones you have been blessed with, Paulie, you would too."

Marlayna leaned forward and pressed a damp palm against Paul's cheek. "I'm scared, Paul. Scared and afraid of what I'm going to hear about myself. Maybe I did fail at being a wife, maybe I even failed at being a woman a man wants to spend the rest of his life with. But I'm also mad. Angry that Noah has found someone else. Was I so easy to replace? He vowed to love, honor and cherish, and I find it offensive that another woman will hear those same words.

"I want justice; I want revenge; I want to shed my guilt. No matter what some judge decreed in five minutes in a courtroom, I am still Noah Drake's wife!"

She tried to control her trembling. "When you were a child, Paul, did you ever play with puzzles?" His silver head nodded. "Well, that's exactly the way my life has been," she told him, "a puzzle that has never been completed, a puzzle that can't even be appreciated because too many pieces are missing."

Paul took a deep breath. "All right, kid, if this is what you really want, I'll back you one hundred percent." His fingers entwined with hers. "I'll even be here to glue all the shattered pieces back together. When is D-Day?"

Sylvia hunted for the engraved card that had slid between the sofa cushions. "Next weekend and . . . oh, look at this note on the back." She turned the card for Marlayna's inspection. "King Arthur's scrawling personal message requests that you spend the entire week at his island castle."

"A week to recapture six years." Marlayna looked from one to the other. "Seems like a fair trade," she said, smiling.

Paul shrugged his shoulders in silent capitulation. "I'll make sure your schedule is free for the next two weeks." At her raised brow, his mouth twisted grimly. "The extra week's just in case Sylvia and I have to play paramedic."

"Doesn't he have a charming way with words?" came Sylvia's caustic pronouncement. "I say we celebrate Marlayna's impending prison break and relocate ourselves to Giovanni's for some antipasto, fettuccine and an aged Burgundy."

"That's the most brilliant idea you've had all week, Sylvia," Paul agreed. "Let's go, Marlayna, and I'll even let you pig out on the sesame bread sticks."

"You two go and gorge," she instructed. "I'd like to be alone for a while and think." Noticing their matching worried expressions, she released an easy laugh. "Hey, I just flew through three time zones! My sneakers are still filled with the California desert and I could use a long soak in a bubble-filled tub."

Sylvia and Paul made their good-byes last another twenty minutes. Once inside the waiting air-conditioned limousine, Paul continued to voice his objections. "We were fools to leave. If we stayed perhaps we could have——"

"Changed her mind?" the blonde inquired. "Paulie, all we would have done was exhaust ourselves and see absolutely no results. Look at things from Marlayna's perspective. She really has no alternative but to confront Noah Drake." Sylvia squeezed Paul's arm. "She knows where she's been for the past six years, but she needs to know what's happened to him and what happened to them. If Marlayna doesn't get the answers, her life will be lived in limbo. Do you want that for her?"

"Of course not! I love that girl." Brown eyes looked into blue. "But, damn it, Sylvie, she's so much better, she should be on top of the world. Do you want to see her come back from Noah Drake the way she was the last time?"

"No, but I honestly don't think Marlayna could ever sink that low again. She's older, stronger, healthier, sharper and in control. We've both seen how she handles herself. On the job, she just tunes out the grinding tedium of the model's routine and virtually ignores all the people that pick and push and poke at her. She handles the never-ending line of fawning males with equal aplomb."

"And you think Marlayna can handle Noah Drake?"

Sylvia nodded. "I think she'll thrive on handling Noah Drake."

"What if your prediction about anticipation being ninety-nine percent of the actual event proves to be true?"

"Then we'll be there to help her."

Paul stared into Sylvia's perfectly made-up face. "She means a lot to you too."

She nodded. "We both know how shallow and materialistic I am, but Marlayna disregarded all of that and kept digging until she found the real human being that is Sylvia Davies."

He ran a hand through shaggily cut silver hair. "Marlayna does have the uncanny ability to ignore surface imperfections and get through to a person's heart."

Sylvia leaned back and let her eyes sweep over him. "You know, Paul, you're really quite a likable, almost lovable, person." One perfectly shaped eyebrow arched in silent appraisal. "I'm very tempted to try and convert you." She lifted the receiver on the rear intercom and spoke to the driver. "Cancel Giovanni's, Fred, and bring us back to my place. Then," winking at Paul, she added, "take the rest of the night off."

There was a quietness about the elegant apartment that Marlayna could feel, a quiet that was neither calming nor soothing nor safe. She left her sneakers at the foot of the Victorian halltree in the foyer and padded barefoot back into the living room.

Her eyes mapped and catalogued her surroundings: the valuable fifteenth-century Italian accent table, a Ming vase here, a signed master's painting there. Brass planters and crystal lamp-bases caught and reflected the coral-tinted sunset; the wall bookcase was filled with hand-tooled leather first editions and a classic eighteenth century French tapestry hung behind glass in the alcove. "It's like living in the Metropolitan Museum of Art," Marlayna sighed.

Living? "Visiting," came her audible correction as she sat in perfect school-girl form on the edge of a Chippendale side chair one step up in the dining room. She had occupied this duplex that Paul had sublet for her for the last three years and still felt like a guest. The only person who took this place seriously was Pearl the housekeeper!

"Perhaps if I had been 'to the manner born.'" Marlayna lifted an invisible cup to her lips, letting her pinky curve in a refined arc. Her fingers opened, letting the phantom china shatter into oblivion. "Face it, kiddo, this house and its furnishings are just not right for you." A melancholy expression shadowed her face and replaced her grin as she remembered a house that was her.

She and Noah had decided to rent one of the remodeled brick pre–World War II bungalows that edged the Georgia Tech campus. They had combined the furniture from their respective apartments, put a fresh coat of paint and new drapes in the rental and discovered that the eclectic mix was charmingly attractive.

"Now that was a home!" Marlayna told the brass unicorn she had lifted from a hand-painted teakwood display pedestal. "My tweed sofa and glass end tables balanced those two leather recliners of Noah's that he put in front of the brick fireplace. His double bed fit the two of us just perfectly and my single set was put in the extra bedroom."

Her eyes inspected the ornate Oriental-style furniture, then looked down at her hands. "How well I remember stripping and staining that oak claw-footed dining table and sideboard we bought at a garage sale."

For the millionth time Marlayna wondered what had happened to all their shared treasures. Anger, fear, confusion and tears had been her only companions when she'd fled Atlanta, and afterward she had let Sylvia's lawyer handle any further communications with Noah's legal representative. There had been a settlement check and the usual signing of documents, but she had been too sick to be interested and Sylvia convinced her that it was beneath her, as a woman, to care.

The trouble was, she did care; she had never stopped caring and wondering and thinking. Always about the past, never about today, no thoughts of tomorrow. "One minute life was simple; the next, so complicated." She inhaled deeply. "Maybe it would have been better if I had taken all of this more seriously." *All of this* included much more than her living quarters.

The fascinating events that changed her life after her divorce from Noah had been more obstructive than constructive. Marlayna had chosen New York City as a place in which to disappear from the face of the earth, but Fate had decided otherwise.

And yet, hadn't she actually become what millions of young women dream of becoming? From obscurity to celebrity—her face and figure were now splashed across fashion pages and magazine covers. Somehow, somewhere, in some other dimension of time, there had been a little mix-up and Marlayna was living someone else's dream.

Her mouth twisted in an impertinent grin. It was really quite funny, *her* dreams had never been filled with fame and fortune. A little cottage, rimmed by a white picket fence, a smiling husband, laughing children and a sleepy schnauzer—that was the stuff *her* dreams had been made of. Dreams that had come true and turned into a nightmare.

But the beginning had been beautiful, she reminisced, the perfect fairy-tale story. She had found her Prince Charming in Noah Drake, or as he had said more correctly, "I've finally found the woman I want to spend the rest of my life with, the woman I want to love and care for and raise children with and grow old with." Marlayna had believed him.

"Why wouldn't I?" she again spoke to the unicorn. "We wanted the same things. We were two alike."

They both had been the only child of only children. If either had aunts, uncles or cousins, their relatives had been well hidden. Her father had suffered a heart attack when she was sixteen and her mother was felled by the same, leaving Marlayna totally on her own at twenty. Noah's parents had been killed in a car accident just after he graduated from high school, and he had let the Marines play surrogate for two tours of duty. At twenty-six he had settled in Atlanta to enter a nonsaluting world.

Noah had been twenty-eight to her twenty-one when they married, and their life together had been a happy one for two years. She was head of admissions in the emergency room but was taking courses at the community college to become a medical lab technician. At the construction company where Noah worked, he was promoted to foreman, but at night he was a student accumulating college credits toward a degree in architecture.

Working and studying had been the main activities for Mr. and Mrs. Noah Drake. Each seemed to thrive on the other's achievements; each needed the other to bolster an ego during a failure; and both reveled in designing their future.

"I am going to build you the house of your dreams." Noah's voice rang fresh in Marlayna's ears.

"The perfect place to live with the man of my dreams," she had said, smiling at him.

"Who's that?"

"You, of course."

"Think so?"

"I know so."

Closing her eyes, her chin resting on the back of the bronze statue that was balanced on her knee, Marlayna easily drifted back in time, back to the last day she had seen her husband.

"For heaven's sake, Noah, stop shouting! It's only the sports page!"

"You could have waited to cut out that coupon, Mimi! Is it too much to ask to read the baseball scores?"

She grabbed the newspaper from the stranglehold

his hand had on it. "I'll tape the damn thing back together."

"Don't bother, I'll read it at work."

"Then why all the fuss?"

Noah had muttered something profane, counted out loud to ten and then picked up his orange hardhat from the dining room table. "Come on, walk me to the door and kiss me good-bye."

"No." Determined arms had folded tightly across the front of her white uniform, building a protective barricade.

"What do you mean 'no'? You know I can't work unless I get a kiss from you." He tried teasing her out of her mood.

"Tough."

"Getting a kiss from you lately has been tough."

"What do you mean by that crack?"

"Oh, hell, Mimi, we can talk about this tonight. I'm going to be late and you already are!"

Marlayna jumped as her mind vividly replayed the slam of the front door six years ago. Six years almost to the day. August thirteenth. A day that, at least to her, would live in infamy. A day on which all dreams and hopes were shattered.

It was four thirty-five on Friday, one half hour to quitting time, and the emergency room at Grady Memorial that had been oddly quiet all day suddenly exploded into activity. Eight ambulances, sirens wailing, screamed into the receiving doors, carrying construction workers who had been caught when a brick wall had suddenly collapsed. Three of the men were red blankets—dead on arrival; five others were in serious condition, one of the five was her husband.

Squeezing her eyes tighter, Marlayna was able to see two Noah Drakes. The first was the half-angry, half-teasing man who had tried and failed to get a good-bye kiss. Six feet of broad-shouldered, tempered muscular strength that had made love to her the first time with such tender care and concern. He had a wonderful smile that reached his brown eyes and a deep cleft in his square chin.

That was the picture of Noah she treasured, the one that remained so disturbingly real that the man actually seemed to have shadowed her all these years. An image so unlike the other one—the one of her husband lying on an ambulance gurney, his body impaled with tubes and wires, his face bruised and bleeding, features distorted by dust and dirt.

She had learned the facts of the accident in the *Atlanta Evening Journal.* Preliminary findings indicated no criminal negligence; the brick wall was reported toppled by a sudden gust of wind. A breeze that instantly extinguished three lives and sent five men to intensive care. Marlayna had ceased being a hospital employee and joined the other wives to wait for word on their husbands.

All received reports but her. None of the nurses or doctors would answer any of her questions; none would even look her in the eye. Finally after over a dozen hours, one doctor did come out and speak.

"Mrs. Drake——"

"How is he? How's my husband?"

"As well as can be expected," was the doctor's vague response. "I think you should go home."

"Home? But I want to see Noah."

"He doesn't want to see you." The physician's hand had squeezed her shoulder. "I'm afraid patient information is not extended to couples who are separated."

"Separated? I . . . what . . . I don't understand."

"Please, Marlayna, just go home. You won't be allowed any extra privileges."

A heavy sigh shook her body. "I never wanted anything extra. Oh, maybe just to give Noah that good-bye kiss he so dearly wanted."

Just a kiss. A simple puckering of two lips pressed against two others. She had longed for that kiss every morning and every evening for six years. Longed for the kiss, longed for the love, longed for the man.

Marlayna's fingers flowed along the sculpted beauty that was the metal unicorn. Unicorn—a mythical beast. Had their happiness been mythical, too? Had all the love, all the laughter, all the sharing, all the caring, all the planning been nothing but a sham?

She chucked the unicorn under his chin. "I bet every divorced woman in the world has asked herself that question and never been able to answer it! Maybe my whole problem is that I cling to the past. Maybe I should say the hell with it all. The hell with Noah Drake. I could always learn to kiss some other man!" Her stomach rumbled in both alarm and annoyance. "Oh hell, maybe I should just get something to eat!" Dragging herself off the chair, she went in search of something more nourishing than shattered dreams and unfulfilled desires.

Her opinion of the duplex's kitchen hadn't altered since the day she had first inspected the rather austere, clinical environment. Marlayna wrinkled her nose at the black leather-look countertops, white wood cabinets and appliances and black and white tile on the floor and walls. She flipped the overhead fluorescent lights on, then quickly turned them off, deciding that her dinner would be much more palatable under the illumination offered by the softer range hood light.

As usual, her housekeeper, Pearl Hardy, had stocked the twenty-four-cubic-foot double-door refrigerator with something from every aisle in the grocery store, and, as usual, Marlayna ignored the wrapped cheeses, the cartons of low-cal yogurt, and the various gourmet deli containers in lieu of her favorite—baloney and mustard—making a major concession in using Pearl's white wine Dijon variety of the condiment.

She unscrewed a jar of pickles and then munched her way through some baby gherkins, while deftly coating slices of diet wheat bread with the brown mustard.

"Don't forget the catsup. I can only eat baloney with mustard and catsup!"

The stainless steel knife fell from suddenly numb fingers, spangling the black countertop yellow brown. "Noah?" Holding a sharply drawn breath, Marlayna whirled around but found that the only companion that haunted the kitchen was a looming stretch of dusk gray shadow that slanted through the west window.

"Take a deep breath and count to ten," she ordered and dutifully followed her own instructions. "This always happens when you think about him. You're fine. There's no reason to call Bellevue and have them send you a straightjacket to model." Marlayna concentrated all her energies on peeling the red wrapper off the luncheon meat.

"You still haven't put on the catsup!"

"There's nobody here who wants catsup," she loudly responded to the deep masculine voice. "There's nobody here but me."

"I'm here. I'm always just behind you."

Marlayna lifted another pickle from the open jar and

spoke to it. "Do you know what's going on? I do. I just spent nine days modeling fur coats in the Mojave Desert, in triple-digit temperatures with two mean, disgustingly smelly camels." Even white teeth snapped through the sweet vegetable. "I'm just having my hallucination a little late. You know how traveling through time zones scrambles one's brain."

"So, I'm just a hallucination."

"Yup." She slapped a piece of bread on top of the baloney. "Just a mirage. A figment of the old imagination."

"Can this figment of your imagination set your body on fire?"

Marlayna felt a warm caress disturb the ebony hair that curled against her nape. She closed her eyes as a sudden flash of heat arced inside her stomach, sending a molten stream of longing snaking slowly downward.

She recalled what it was like to touch and be touched by Noah. The feeling came back fresh and alive. Her lips were too sensitive, nerve endings all exposed; her nipples grew hard, pushing urgently against the soft sweatshirt material of her jacket.

Noah wasn't even here, yet he could so easily seduce her—easily, artfully, creatively, imaginatively. He touched her in her dreams each night. All the memories kept coming home—everything had come back—everything but Noah Drake.

Swallowing convulsively, her tongue washed around a dry mouth. "I'm afraid, dear phantom, that you can set me on fire. You know you've been a wonderful fantasy lover for the last six years. But that will soon come to an end."

"I'm still owed that kiss, Mimi."

Snapping off the meager range hood light, Marlayna took her sandwich in one hand and the jar of pickles in the other. "Next week, you can have your kiss." She elbowed open the black cafe doors and, without looking back into the shadows, added: "I may owe you a kiss, Noah Drake, but you owe me a baby."

3

⬤◦◦◦◦◦◦◦◦◦◦⬤

Here's that sexy new perfume you requested." The heel of Sylvia Davies's taupe lizard skin sandal kicked Marlayna's apartment door closed. "I couldn't believe it when you called and actually *asked* for something." She held out the petite monogrammed Lord & Taylor shopping bag. "Especially when something, even with my discount, comes to one hundred dollars an ounce!"

Marlayna laughed at Sylvia's bobbing eyebrows. "I finally begin to spend a few bucks and everybody gets apoplexy." She linked their arms. "You should have heard Paul when I asked to keep some of the lingerie wardrobe I modeled Wednesday."

"That's because this new you is such a sudden transformation. You've never spent money on anything but the bare essentials, and you've always tried to refuse or return pre-offered clothing. Now in the space of a week—" Her right hand made a fluttering gesture, then returned to pat Marlayna's arm. "Oh, well, I've always wanted to see a caterpillar explode from the cocoon and try butterfly wings."

"That's another reason I asked you to come." Marlayna led Sylvia into the crisp white decorator master bedroom. "I'm not quite sure what this novice butterfly should pack for tomorrow's flight."

Sylvia's amber eyes blinked at the confused jumble of clothing that nearly obliterated the pink rosebuds that bloomed across the white satin comforter. "I see that you like to work in a state of controlled hysteria."

Marlayna blanched, her skin defying its sun-toasted tan to turn ash gray.

"Hey!" Sylvia pressed her into a seated position on the tapestry footbench and pushed her head between her knees. "Come on, sweetie, don't faint." She bent to inspect Marlayna's color. "That's better. What happened?"

"That word." Marlayna murmured and then sat up. "Hysteria." She took two deep breaths. "A neurosis whose victims appear calm on the surface but suffer from hallucinations, mental aberrations and uncontrollable fear and panic." Her mouth made a feeble attempt at a smile. "I looked it up. That's me. Ms. Hysteria."

"But Paul said your shooting schedule this past week included the best work you've ever done."

"My face has been lying to the camera," came her sighing rejoinder. Haunted eyes latched onto Sylvia's confused expression. "I'm getting very good at lying, my dear friend—lying without ever having to say a word."

Sylvia settled on a second bench at the foot of the

king-size bed. "I'm not quite sure what to do. Should I slip out into the kitchen on the pretext of making tea and call the men in the white coats? Or should I just sit and listen?"

Marlayna smiled. "Sit and listen and then make tea and call the men in the white coats." She balanced her elbows on denim-covered knees, fingers folded under her chin. "I've . . . I've been talking to Noah."

"You called him?"

"Uh . . . no."

"He called you?"

"No."

"Hmmmm . . . I don't quite understand."

"That's the hallucination and mental aberrations part."

"How do you like your tea?"

She turned her head toward Sylvia. "You think I'm crazy."

Amber eyes flicked over an anxious face. "No, I don't. As I recall, I once shared my bed with three rather vivid specters that were George, Sam and Brian. Sam took the longest to get rid of, damn him. I kept whipping up biscuits, making each batch flakier than the last, and leaving them on the kitchen table with the butter and honey he'd asked for. And do you know, those biscuits would be gone."

At Marlayna's silent inquiry, Sylvia shook her head. "He wasn't eating them; I was. Only I never remembered doing it until my bathroom scale registered five pounds more!" Her index finger tapped against her temple. "The brain is an interesting organ, much more powerful than the heart or the glands. Do you mind if I ask you a few questions?"

"Shoot."

"What is it you fear the most?"

"Finding out that Noah never loved me and our marriage was a sham."

"Can this happen?"

"Yes."

Sylvia hesitated a moment. "If it actually does happen, what is the worst result?"

Marlayna opened her mouth, then closed it. "Well . . . I guess . . ." Her hands slapped her thighs as she straightened her spine. "I guess the worst has happened—divorce."

"Then that takes care of that particular fear. Any other fears?"

"Gwen Kingman."

"The lipstick princess?" Sylvia laughed. "Come on, you must be joking."

"Have you ever met her?"

Sylvia nodded.

A shaky hand rumpled ebony curls. "Is she"— Marlayna swallowed around the rapidly growing lump that blocked her throat—"Is she charming? Special? Desirable? Attractive?"

"Yes. To her father. Not particularly. Maybe." The platinum blonde reached to grab her friend's hand. "She's twenty-three, Marlayna, a very young twenty-three. An adolescent who giggles and gushes and goshes. Who bounces and bubbles and brags. When King Arthur's not waxing lyrical about his antiwrinkle cream, he waxes about his little princess."

"She sounds nice."

Sylvia shrugged. "So who wants nice?"

"Apparently Noah."

"And you want Noah." A peremptory palm was held up. "I'm getting dizzy!" Sylvia recreased the knife-edged pleats on her red and white patterned silk dress. "You know, Marlayna, you can't force a man to love you."

She stood up and surveyed the clothes that littered the bed. "I realize that."

"Do you also realize Noah could actually be in love with Gwen Kingman?" Marlayna nodded. "You know there are other men out there. Look at me," Sylvia joked, "I found Mr. Right three times!"

"I found him too." Marlayna lifted a white negligee that was draped across the pillows and a black lace teddie that hung from the French Provincial headboard. "Should I be nice or try for naughty?" she inquired. "This was the same dilemma I had when I packed for my honeymoon."

"Honeymoon!" Sylvia echoed sharply. "You're not going on any damn honeymoon!" Lunging to her feet, she snatched the silken lingerie out of Marlayna's hand and threw it back on the bed. "What makes you think Noah and Gwen haven't already taken a pre-honeymoon honeymoon of their own?"

Ignoring her friend's stricken face, Sylvia went on ruthlessly. "I was convinced that you had yourself all together, that you had matured and grown strong. But I find that I was wrong. You are one very vulnerable lady when it comes to Noah Drake." She inhaled sharply and continued.

"Do you think two people become engaged because they *hate* each other? So she's thirteen years younger than he is—maybe he's trying to recapture his youth. Who knows what the hell a man thinks! And"—Sylvia's small breasts heaved—"and did you even stop to consider that after six years, Noah Drake may look like a goddamn toad!"

After a minute's silence, Marlayna's dry, slightly whimsical voice returned: "Don't be ridiculous. King Arthur would have slathered wart cream all over Noah's body."

Blue gray eyes held gilded brown ones, traded a wink, and then companionable laughter conquered the anger that had built up.

"Maybe hysteria is contagious," Sylvia said, shaking her head to clear it as she settled next to Marlayna on the bed. "I apologize." Her fingers squeezed her friend's shoulder. "I shouldn't have trespassed into your dreams."

"I'm glad you did," Marlayna returned at length. Her head lowered, eyes making a study of the pink cotton weave on her shirt. "I've spent the past week living in a fantasy world, talking with and laughing with and loving a man who wasn't even here." Marlayna cast a sardonic glance at Sylvia. "I'm afraid that doesn't say too much for the maturity of my mind."

The blonde issued a noncommittal hum as the brunette continued to speak. "It's funny how the mind does work. I find myself playing a very vivid part in different scenarios with Noah. Words, actions, promises—everything is so perfect."

Sylvia looked at her quizzically. "It sounds like you have more in mind than just getting questions answered."

"I do."

"What?"

"A baby."

"Baby? A baby! So that's what you're really after." She stood up and faced her. "You are crazy." Each word was enunciated with force.

Pacing back and forth, hands flailing, Sylvia tried to

assemble a coherent argument. "I know how tragic that miscarriage was for you. But Marlayna, you can't replace the loss of one baby with the birth of another."

"I know——"

"I'm not sure you *know* a damn thing!" Sylvia ran an agitated hand around the back of her neck, and her palm came away damp and sticky. "So you're going on this weekend with every intention of coming back pregnant. What happens if Noah isn't interested? Are you going to rape him?"

She didn't allow time for an answer. "Hell, why would you even want to have sex with a man who didn't love you, let alone carry his child?"

"Because I love him," she spoke with conviction.

"You're in love with a memory, not a man. He's got to have changed. You have." Sylvia's fingers wrapped around Marlayna's wrists, pulling her to stand in front of the cheval glass. "Take a good look." Her palm pushed up a lowered chin. "Keep looking," she instructed, pressing Marlayna closer to the mirror. "Is this the same twenty-one-year-old girl who dithered over what to pack on her honeymoon?" Sylvia stepped carefully out of the reflection. "I'm going to make us a pot of strong tea and some sandwiches. Maybe if you look into yourself for a while, you'll come up with a few answers of your own."

Marlayna's immediate answer was one of defiance. She reclaimed the fragile white nightgown. As she held it tight against her body, one hand positioned the fragile lace bodice in proper place over her cotton T-shirt and the other hand fanned the floor-length skirt for inspection.

The dreamy expression and sublime smile on her face was duplicated on her mirrored image. "This is almost like the one I wore on my wedding night." She lovingly fingered the luxurious satin material. "I bought seven gowns, one for each night of the honeymoon. There was bridal white, pink, lilac, blue, green, fiery red and"—she took a step backward and picked up the teddie—"the last was sultry black."

Humming gently, Marlayna whirled and twirled and swirled in front of the looking glass until she lost her balance, stumbled backward and collapsed across the clothes-strewn bed. "Ohh . . . ooh." Her eyelids fluttered shut, exchanging the revolving room for soothing blackness. In doing so, she closed a window on the present and opened one on the past.

She found herself in surroundings quite different from the duplex's arctic white master bedroom, and she wasn't alone. "Heavens, those brochures certainly didn't exaggerate about the honeymoon villas in the Poconos," her audibly nervous voice exclaimed. "Everything is red and white. Gosh, Noah, look at the round bed and . . . the . . . the bathtub *is* heart-shaped!"

"You're going a little red, yourself, Mimi." His deep masculine voice turned her nickname into an endearment.

Marlayna stammered and babbled her way out of the bathroom. "Why don't I just unpack us and——"

"Why don't we just shake the dust off that bed." Noah's hands settled on either side of the green suitcase she was in the process of lifting and settled it back on the red carpet. "Hey, what's the matter, love?" Wrapping his arms around her waist, he nuzzled the side of her neck with his cheek. "I do believe you're scared of your new husband."

"You're right. I am. Sort of. . . ." She took a deep steadying breath and searched inside herself, hoping to find a vein of cool, clever sophistication. Instead, she discovered a steadily increasing passion for the man who was holding her. "Mmmm . . . what are you doing?"

"It's the Noah Drake method for effectively combatting the new wife jitters."

With a more relaxed sigh, she leaned closer against him, luxuriating under the lengthy strokes his hands were making along her spine. "How many new wives have you stopped jittering?"

His lips languidly sculpted the rounded curve of her jaw and settled by her ear. "You're my first wife," Noah admitted in a husky whisper. "First, last and always. Have I told you lately how much I love you?"

"Not for at least five minutes." She suddenly became very involved with his body. She pushed beneath the silken knit of his gray shirt, fingers pressing into the lean muscled strength of his shoulders. His flesh was hard and tough. When her hands slid around to his chest, the dark crisp hairs trapped her eagerly exploring fingertips. The spicy smell of him aroused her, as did Noah's own investigating hands.

She felt the zipper lowering on the back of her pale yellow sundress and then the wide ribbon straps were discreetly untied. Noah pressed butterfly kisses along her right cheekbone and on the tip of her nose, his lips coming to a gentle rest against hers.

"Do you know I only started breathing, really feeling alive the day I was lucky enough to meet you."

The sincerity of his words and the timbre of his voice made her eyes pool with tears. "Oh, Noah, I feel the same." Marlayna's arms moved to encircle his neck. "I love you very much and I'm not afraid anymore."

"Suddenly I am." His brown gaze darkened seriously. "I want everything to be perfect for you. Today, tomorrow and always. And I want to be perfect for you. You deserve nothing less."

"So . . ."—she pressed closer, her rounded feminine form filling in the rough angles of his male physique—"perfect me . . ." Her mouth settled warmly, firmly, enticingly onto his.

Noah masterfully accepted her invitation. His tongue was a playful intruder that teased apart her lips and probed the lush interior beyond. Dual sighs and moans echoed softly and were alternately provoked and ravenously consumed by nibbling teeth, rubbing lips and cavorting tongues.

Assorted masculine and feminine clothes began to clutter the ruby carpet until each stood viewing the other wrapped in a shared cloak of love. "You are incredibly beautiful, Mrs. Drake." Noah's arms moved around the indentation of her waist, his large hands settling low to cup the rounded globes of her buttocks.

"You, Mr. Drake, certainly surpass any naked man I've ever seen," Marlayna whispered, her teeth pulling at his earlobe.

"How many naked men have you seen, love?"

She shivered in delightful anticipation as his right hand moved upward, across her torso to gently cup her full breast. "Ooo . . . only one in a rather risqué R-rated movie and a copy of Michelangelo's *David.*"

"So, I'm better than an Italian master's statue?" His thumb and forefinger deftly manipulated the hardened nipple.

Her palm moved slowly down his sinewy chest, fingers splaying amid the silken mat of dark curls. "You're much, much better," Marlayna told him truthfully. "You're flesh and blood and very, very real." Her hand slid lower. "Although it seems one very intrinsic part of you is growing marble hard."

"And very anxious." He lowered his head, letting his lips and tongue take the place of his fingers. She felt electrified and whimpered with pleasure, wondering how it was possible to constrict with delicious tension one minute and suddenly feel that all her bones had been turned to gelatin the next.

"Noah . . . please . . ." Marlayna was surprised to hear herself begging. "Please . . . I don't think I can stand up any longer. . . ."

"That makes two of us, love." He led her to the massive round bed that readily provided support. Noah spangled her velvety breasts with a hundred kisses. His coarse tongue reverently bathed a painfully taut nipple before his aggressive mouth gently suckled.

Sweet sensations moved along her nerves to her heart—a heart that was pounding against her husband's, her lover's. His caressing hand ventured lower, drifting like a gentle breeze across her belly, the tip of his finger making a tender intrusion into the moist core of her femininity.

"Relax, darling, relax. I won't hurt you."

Her hands cradled either side of his face. Love-filled eyes worshiped his every feature. "I trust you, Noah, my husband. Trust you and love you and—"

A mind-jarring crash jerked Marlayna to a sitting position as Sylvia's voice caroled, "Don't worry, it was just an odd glass. I'm making two cheese omelets instead of sandwiches. They'll be done in ten minutes."

Marlayna swallowed convulsively and tried to reorient herself to this room, this place, this year. The six-foot mirror reflected her flushed features and the limp form that she resolutely dragged off the bed. A shaky hand further tangled damp sable curls. "How can he keep doing this to me? How can one person hold on so tight, so long, and so thoroughly to another? Am I mentally ill? Or am I a woman still in love with her husband?"

There didn't seem to be an answer to any of the questions that she was asking. "Questions!" Her nose wrinkled in disgust. "Why is my damn life filling up with more questions?" A tremulous laugh bubbled as she added yet another question.

"Mind over matter. Mind over matter." She kept up the chant as she neatened her twisted shirt and straightened her jeans. Marlayna moved to the white tufted boudoir chair and snapped on the lights that rimmed the makeup mirror. A natural bristle brush restored order to her hair, and the contents of various pots and bottles concealed the dark circles under her eyes and toned down the blush that seemed to have indelibly stained her cheeks.

In a matter of minutes, she was her old, composed self. At least on the outside. "This face lies so easily." A worried sigh escaped her. Maybe the Fates had chosen the perfect occupation for her. How easily she was able to compose and calculate and pretend both in front of the camera and off. No matter how shattered she was on the inside, everyone always raved about how wonderful she looked.

Just maybe—she gazed at herself for a long moment—maybe that bit of talent would enable her to get through the weekend and the week ahead. She'd have to be a woman of many faces—one for Arthur Kingman, one for his daughter Gwen and another for Noah Drake.

Noah. How could the sound of a name make her feel so many things? Her clenched fist hit the top of the marble table, making assorted cosmetics jump and topple. "Damn you, Noah! Why can't you let me live in peace? What is it you have that spoiled me for any other man?"

Marlayna looked herself straight in the eye. "This has got to stop. No more fantasy lover. No more dreams of yesterday. No more scripting the perfect scene." She reached out and patted the cheek of her image. "Let's not start playing the game until all the cards have been dealt. Win, lose or draw, you certainly can't become any worse than you already are." She stood up and headed for the door, pausing to add over her shoulder, "And just maybe you might come out ahead."

"Perfect timing." Sylvia looked up from pouring the coffee as Marlayna entered the kitchen. "You look a little better. Are you?"

She favored her friend with a genuine smile. "I've decided to approach this little outing on another level. After dinner, I'll let you help me pack clothes suitable for a castle warming and a minivacation on an island in the St. Lawrence."

Sylvia's responding smile was smug. "Now that's a much more mature, sensible attitude."

Marlayna reached for a slice of buttered diet wheat toast. "Thank you, I'm trying." Even white teeth snapped a healthy bite of bread.

"To be exact, there are one thousand eight hundred and thirty-four islands," Captain Warren readily answered Marlayna's question. "The Indians called the St. Lawrence 'river without end' and it's populated by beautiful wooded islands that the French named *Les Milles Iles* or Thousand Islands."

Looking out the wide port windows, she saw islands

that ranged from no more than rocks to others that were verdant land masses dotted with homesites. "The islands certainly are beautiful," she agreed.

"A million-dollar playground with the first five-and-ten-cent store." The captain recited a paraphrased version of an old song. He laughed embarrassedly, and at her quizzical look explained further.

"During the late eighteen hundreds the rich and celebrated came to relax in the great stone mansions and luxury hotels that populated the islands. Frank W. Woolworth also came, setting up his first mercantile store in Watertown. Today, it's a boater's dream holiday to tour the 'jewels in the crown of the Empire State.' "

His deeply tanned complexion bore the unmistakable imprint of weathering by sea and sun. "Is this your first trip to the castle?"

Marlayna nodded. "My first boat trip too."

"In that case, if you'll excuse me for a moment, I'll instruct the bridge to slow us down so I can give you the five-and-ten-cent tour."

She gave the captain a relieved smile as she patted her stomach. But to be truthful, her butterflies had been in evidence long before the launch left Blind Bay Marina and passed Chippewa Point doing fifteen knots.

Her blue gray eyes matched the arrogant St. Lawrence and the river's whitecapped choppiness echoed her own tremulous emotions. Marlayna's chaotic feelings suddenly threatened her ability to breathe and to stand, making her stumble into the comfort of a nearby deck chair.

She felt like a tightrope walker, wondering how far was too far. How much longer would it take for her to falter and completely lose her very delicate balance? Trembling fingers wiped the perspiration off her upper lip. It's amazing, Marlayna thought, how the man I love most in the world is suddenly the man I fear the most.

"Here we are." Captain Warren's voice interrupted her musings. "Thought this might help." He handed her a tall plastic ice-filled glass of bubbling crystal liquid garnished with lemon wedges. "Would you mind if I joined you? It's quite a luxury for me to get a single passenger to entertain."

"I'd be honored." She took a healthy swallow and found the crisp tonic water refreshing. "This hits the spot. Thank you." Marlayna flashed him a smile. "Am I your first passenger to the island or the last?" She looked pointedly at eighteen unoccupied chairs.

"One hundred thirty passengers preceded you, Miss O'Brian," the captain acknowledged, "and there'll be a few more after you." Seeing the condensation from the glass begin to drip onto her white slacks, he hurriedly pulled a small table closer to her. "Mr. Kingman hired both of my charter launches this weekend to transport his guests."

An impressed expression settled on her face. "I hadn't realized the castle was large enough to accommodate so many people."

"We'll be returning the majority of them back to either the marina or to hotels on other islands." He relaxed more comfortably in his chair. "I'm not going to spoil the surprise of your seeing the castle on Jorstadt, but I will say it could easily house that many visitors."

Marlayna's dark head nodded starboard. "I've been noticing a lot of river traffic. Tramp steamers?"

"Ore and grain boats heading for Montreal and on to Europe. We cross the main shipping channel." He was interrupted by a loud honking and directed Marlayna's attention toward the rapidly-moving V-shaped formation that was visible off the stern. "Snow geese. The islands have the largest population in the world."

For another twenty minutes Captain Warren regaled Marlayna with amusing river tales and some rather disputable fishing yarns that involved the annual "muskie" derbies—involving the wily native game fish called muskellunge that reach over five feet in length and weigh upward of seventy pounds. "Honest"—his palm was held up—"before you leave Blind Bay, you take a peek inside Sam's Fish House. That muskie's mounted right over the door."

"I will." She shook her finger in warning. "But I bet this fish doubles in size every time you tell about it."

His laughter mingled with hers. "Triples." Captain Warren's blue gaze shifted over her shoulder to the flashing red channel marker. "If you'll excuse me." He stood and touched the brim of his hat. "Duty calls. We're getting ready to head into the docking area on Jorstadt."

The lighthearted pleasure she had succumbed to, courtesy of the captain, was instantly replaced by the familiar anxiety. Marlayna inhaled deeply, counted to ten and reached for her purse. "Let's check on our happy face" came her mumbled directive.

A fresh coat of pearlized copper was applied to her lips; powder daubed on forehead, nose and chin eliminated their shine; and she valiantly tried to blink away the haunted, intimidated look that clouded her eyes. Standing, she smoothed the legs of her pleated white trousers and tilted up the collar of her short-sleeved indigo silk blouse.

Her reflection shimmered in the thick wall of Lexan that protected the launch's passengers from wind and sea spray. "Cool and confident." Marlayna fluffed out the ebony curls that tumbled to her eyebrows and then smoothed any errant waves behind her ears and along her nape. Her fingernail flicked the gold loop that dangled from her left earlobe; even she was narcissistically impressed.

"Ahoy, *Lady of the Lakes.*"

"Ahoy, Jorstadt. We're carrying one very beautiful passenger."

Marlayna stepped out of the shielded area onto the deck, watching as the disembarking ramp was expertly lowered into place. Standing in front of a generously proportioned redwood belvedere was Arthur King-man. For a long moment, she took in the tall, lean frame that was elegantly cloaked in designer jeans and a pink golf shirt; then, with a resigned sigh, she waved a greeting before turning to extend her hand to Captain Warren. "Thank you for a wonderful voyage."

His left palm added an extra measure of pressure over their clasped hands. "Thank you for enduring and laughing at my sea stories. Your luggage will be given to the porter, and now, regretfully, I must give you to King Arthur." His right eyelid closed in a merry wink.

Arthur Kingman couldn't wait for his guest's white espadrilles to hit the dock. His long legs quickly conquered the distance that kept them separated. "Marlayna, I was praying you hadn't stood me up."

She deftly avoided the masculine arms that were

trying to surround her waist. "Arthur"—her hands captured his—"it's so lovely to see you again." Marlayna also succeeded in outmaneuvering his lips, making his kiss slide off her jaw. "I'm afraid the lateness of my arrival is due to the airlines. The plane was late from Albany to Ogdensburg."

Taking a step back, she gave him a well-rehearsed, beaming smile. "I see both island and castle life agree with you; you look wonderful."

"Speaking of looking wonderful . . ." Arthur managed to wiggle his left hand free and caress the delicate shadow beneath her cheek. "Marlayna"—the timbre of his voice deepened over each syllable of her name—"do you know how much joy you've brought me this year, and right this moment. I——"

"Arthur, what a sweet sentiment!" She purposely kept her tone light and breezy. "I'm so anxious to see your fabulous castle." Marlayna linked her arm companionably around his and began to venture further along the dock. "This summer house is certainly a classic beginning."

Frowning slightly, he ran his fingers through the thick sandy hair generously veined with silver. This always happens whenever I try to get closer, Arthur mused. I wish I knew the words that would open Marlayna O'Brian to me. "We do enjoy the gazebo on these lazy, sultry summer nights," he finally responded, leading her along a stone path through a dense grove of towering maple trees and fragrant evergreens.

"Tell me more about the castle," she invited, shuffling through the brown pine needles that threatened to obscure most of the granite steps.

"You'll be getting your first breathtaking view right"

—he hesitated while they climbed another four steps —"now!"

Marlayna's gasp was genuine. "Breathtaking is the perfect word! My goodness, Arthur, you own one big *pink* castle."

His deep laugh echoed through the forest. "It's the biggest, most romantic *pink* elephant on the St. Lawrence," Arthur conceded with a grin. "The bell tower is five stories; there are two huge boat houses on the far docks; forty-six bedrooms and an indoor squash court which now accommodates my tennis skills. The interior is filled with suits of armor, medieval weapons, a mix of eighteenth and twentieth century furniture plus a maze of secret passages."

She cleared her throat and tried to figure out what question to ask first. "I can see the drawbridge now and a fortress wall around the moat." Marlayna spoke to him, but her eyes were still occupied by the sheer spectacle of the structure. "Arthur, how long have you been building this place?"

"I wish I could take the credit," he returned, "but the castle was built in 1896 by Frederick G. Bourne, the Singer sewing machine magnate. He imported nearly ninety Italian stonemasons who worked on the rose-hued granite for eight years. Most of the island's ten acres are in New York State, but a small corner is in Canada."

Arthur's hand cupped her right elbow as he resumed walking. "I have spent the last two years and considerable sums of money maintaining and restoring the castle. All the accolades deservedly go to the architect that handled the project, Noah Drake. He's a wonderful man, and I'm thrilled that he and my Gwen are engaged."

Marlayna's foot skidded on the drawbridge, her right ankle twisted and, if it hadn't been for Arthur Kingman's helpful hand, she would have stumbled and thrashed her way into a lily-pad-dotted moat.

"Are you all right?" He stooped to brush the dirt off the knee of her white pants.

"Fine. Really." She managed to calm her erratic breathing. "As you can see, I'm more Thumbelina than ballerina."

Arthur took advantage of Marlayna's embarrassment by snaking his arm around her waist. "This will provide you with a bit more security." Looking over his shoulder, he gave a cursory glance at the wide wooden planks. "I'll have one of the groundskeepers check on that bridge. Won't do to have an accident."

A dozen steps later found them facing two mammoth arched wooden doors. Arthur Kingman pushed against a round brass plate, engraved with his coat of arms. "Noah had this researched and fitted as a castle-warming present."

"Very impressive," she agreed, taking the proper amount of time to appreciate the heraldry. A gold crown was centered between two gold halberds, or battle axes, that were crossed on a shield of red. Marlayna's gaze lowered as she translated the Latin motto: Omnia Vincit Amor—love conquers all. "Very, very nice." It was trite but all she could manage.

With a chivalrous half-bow, Arthur motioned her inside. "Welcome to Kingman Castle." The massive reception hall was cool and empty. "Right now all my guests are playing golf or tennis, swimming, boating, relaxing or just snooping around."

"Hmmm . . . I can certainly see how snooping around could become a habit here." She ran her

61

fingers down the cold arm of a six-foot suit of armor that stood guard by the stone staircase. "Goodness, Arthur, I don't know what to look at first."

His responding smile was one of pure pleasure. "Well, you'll have an entire week to snoop, my dear." Arthur's hand slid around her shoulders to bestow an intimate squeeze. "And in that week I want to take some time for the two of us to get better acquainted. You know, Marlayna"—his gray eyes narrowed on her face—"I'm a little concerned; Paul Wingate has yet to act on the new contract that I've offered you."

If there was any one single thing that had put Marlayna off Arthur Kingman, it was the cruel twist to his lips when he didn't get his own way. Cruel. Yes, that was a word that at times was the key to describing the cosmetic king.

Marlayna was smart enough to know that this man needed to be handled with the "kiddest" of gloves. She didn't want to be insulting, so she decided to be charming and evasive. "Now, Arthur"—her husky contralto strove to soothe—"since when did you start mixing business with pleasure?"

She knew that she had gained the advantage when his military stance suddenly drooped and his eyes no longer stared into hers. She continued, "I'm sure you didn't know that just two weeks ago I was on a hot, dusty, exhausting assignment in the Mojave. And last week I did double duty, just so I could spend some extra time here." Marlayna gave an inward wince as she tapped her index finger in the deep cleft of his chin. "Paul and I haven't even had time to discuss the new contract."

Quickly he caught her hand and pressed a warm kiss into her palm. "I apologize. You must think me an insensitive brute." His eyes darkened as they hungered over her every feature. "But I am very, very determined not to let you slip away."

Her attempt at a smile was feeble. There was no denying the threat underlying his statement. Marlayna turned the conversation back to her surroundings. "Arthur, what a magnificent carpet."

"Thank you. I picked that up in Iran some years ago. The soft blending of red and gold is warm and welcoming, and I do like the 'tree of life' motif." Arthur suddenly slapped his cheek. "God, what a fool! Here I am making you stand around. Let's go into the lounge area and relax with a drink. Or perhaps you'd like to go to your room and freshen up? Maybe change and take a swim? Or——"

He was interrupted by the opening of an elevator door at the far end of the entry hall. "Hi, Daddy." A dark-haired young woman wiggled her hand in greeting. "Noah and I are headed for the pool. There's a half dozen phone messages for you and . . ."

Marlayna was no longer listening to the rapid-fire exchange between father and daughter. Her eyes were riveted on the tall dark-haired man standing next to Gwen Kingman. A man she hadn't seen in six years but still knew intimately. A man named Noah Drake.

4

≈━⦁⦁⦁⦁⦁⦁⦁⦁⦁⦁━≈

She took him by surprise. In fact, he didn't really notice her until she took a step out of Arthur Kingman's shadow and made herself completely visible. Even then Noah Drake found himself unsure.

Perhaps it was only an optical illusion. A mix of his imagination and the sun's rays slanting through the stained glass ovals that flanked the main door. His brown eyes concentrated on a figure that was cast in a hazy, colorful retrospect. He kept staring at her face, anxiously trying to corroborate all the evidence.

Then the elevator door began its languid sweep to the right. Slowly and steadily the metal block began to wipe her from his view, but, undaunted, Noah flowed with the movement. Leaning from the waist, he slid just as slowly and steadily until the door bounced shut. Then his right shoulder slammed into the wall, his damp palm slipped from the handle of his cane and he found himself flailing to regain his balance.

"Noah!" Gwen made a grab for the raglan sleeve on his yellow beach jacket. "What happened? Are you hurt?" She expended considerable energy trying to help him straighten up. "Did . . . did you break anything?"

"No. I . . . uh . . ." He took a deep breath and realigned both his body and his fractured thoughts. "It was nothing. Really." Noah exchanged embarrassment for annoyance. "Gwen, I've repeatedly told you that I'm neither a piece of Dresden china nor an invalid."

"I'm . . . I'm sorry." Her whispered apology was barely audible as the elevator doors clanked open on the heavily populated indoor pool grotto. "Please"—she placed her hand on his bicep—"don't be mad at me again. I know you were upset when you discovered Daddy had turned the housewarming into a surprise engagement party but——"

"I'm *upset* about this damn engagement, period," came his taut rejoinder. Taking her elbow, Noah guided her into a sheltered area away from the loudly festive crowd. "It's usually the man who proposes, Gwen. You've really got me in a corner about this whole thing."

"So you keep saying."

"That's because I still don't remember how this mushroomed."

Her brown eyes shifted under his narrowed gaze. "Well . . . you were in one of those black moods of yours . . . having trouble reworking that design on the boat house Daddy insisted on, and your back was giving you a problem and . . . well . . . we were sitting and drinking that night and . . . I . . . just . . . sort of . . ." Ten magenta-painted toenails scratched against the pebbled decking as Gwen's voice trailed off.

"That probably means I was a few scotches over my limit," Noah finished. His disgusted tone was meant to encompass them both. A weary hand rubbed his face, then moved to the back of his neck to try and massage away the dull ache that had developed during the last ten minutes. "Look, Gwen, you and I are going to have to sit down and discuss a few things."

"You keep saying that, too."

That whining tone she could so quickly manufacture grated in his ears. "I've been saying it for the last six weeks, and you've consistently and persistently been flitting off for parts and places unknown and avoiding me."

Gwen's expression was sullen, her tone peremptory. "*Now* is hardly the time, Noah." Her hand made an all-encompassing gesture. "I do have an obligation to entertain Daddy's guests. After all, I am his hostess and"—a neatly arched eyebrow lifted—"did you forget that you are *the* honored guest?"

"The castle is the honored guest."

She sucked in her cheeks. "I hate it when you get cynical." Gwen turned her face away and chewed on her lower lip while her fingers played with her long dark braid. "What gets into you, anyway? A few minutes ago you were just fine and now you're . . . you're like a volcano ready to erupt. And men have the nerve to say we women have moods!" She blinked rapidly, trying to stall tears that came both from anger and fear. "I love you, Noah, and I know you like me." Gwen sniffed. "That'll be enough."

Noah found that it was his turn to look the other way. He shuffled his body backward, not stopping until the solid presence of a marble colonnade was felt against his spine and legs. God, how could he have let himself get tangled in this web?

His dark gaze shifted to study a petulant Gwen. She had arrived on May Day, fresh from the Sorbonne and determined to show off various degrees in art by decorating the castle. Noah had found her more child than woman, always in the mood to sulk; her mouth naturally formed a pout. He should have kept his distance but couldn't. The reason: Arthur Kingman's twenty-three-year-old daughter bore a remarkable resemblance to his wife.

Wife! Noah's smooth forehead rippled in concentration; that woman certainly looked like his Mimi. Then again, maybe he just wanted her to. No. There were too many striking similarities, or were there? This woman had short hair and was much slimmer than his wife and yet . . .

Noah cleared his throat and tried to sound casual. "Gwen, who was that in the hallway with your father? Another magazine reporter?"

She moved closer to him, her hands playing with the zipper on his poplin jacket. "So that's what set you off?" Gwen gave a relieved sigh. "You shouldn't get so uptight about giving interviews. What's one more picture? One more recitation? You're going to have to get used to it, Noah. Daddy loves press coverage."

"Was it another reporter?" he persisted.

"To tell you the truth, I didn't really get a good look." She gave him a wide smile. "Could have been. Daddy's like a cat on a hot tin roof, himself. Won't tell me anything. Although I did see a letter from *Architectural Digest*. What a coup for you both!"

"Yeah. I suppose." His fingers fanned through the dark hair at his temples. "Maybe I'll just go back upstairs and take a look-see."

"But . . . but I thought we were going for a swim."
Gwen quickly shrugged off her white terry cover-up.
"I'm wearing my new bikini." Her lashes fluttered
suggestively.

"Nice." Noah gave her well-rounded figure a curso-
ry inspection, then patted her head. "You go and see if
those little scraps of white fabric can handle water."
He limped a wide circle around her scantily clad body.
"I'll be back in a while, unless of course it is the *Digest*.
At any rate"—his finger pressed the elevator button—
"I'll see you at the cocktail party on the back patio
before dinner."

When he finally reached the entrance hall, Noah
found it empty. He hobbled into the nearest lounge
but found that that, too, was unoccupied. The prospect of checking over one hundred rooms and ten
acres made him decide to ring for the head of the
household staff. The house manager promptly responded. "Perkins, could you tell me what happened
to the dark-haired, attractive woman who arrived
about"—Noah checked his watch—"ummm . . .
twenty minutes ago with Mr. Kingman?"

"I wasn't in attendance at that time, sir." The regal,
impeccably dressed Englishman was thoughtful for a
moment. "Let me do a bit of checking. Will you wait in
here?"

"Yes." He collapsed into an antique Shepherd's
Crook open armchair and laid his cane across the top
of his thighs.

Perkins looked concerned. "May I get you something, sir? Perhaps a drink?"

"Yes. Ah . . . no. I . . . uh . . . may need a double
later though."

"Very good, sir."

In less than three minutes, Perkins returned. "A Miss

O'Brian was the new arrival, sir. She's retired to the Queen Anne suite in the west wing."

Miss O'Brian. Noah exhaled a pent-up breath. "And where is Mr. Kingman?"

"On the phone in the library."

"Thank you, Perkins. Fine job as usual."

The butler nodded, took one step, then halted. "Will you be needing that double now, sir?"

"Not just yet, Perkins, and depending on how things go, I may need a triple."

Marlayna stared up at the elaborately ruched and swagged pink taffeta bed canopy and decided that the Queen Anne suite was well named—it did make one feel regal. Pastel elegance was everywhere—from the delicate pink tones that softened the blue pattern in the antique French wallpaper panels to the tiles that framed the fireplace hearth, the softly blended shades in the Persian carpet and the pale roses inlaid in the Louis XV rococo furnishings.

The nicest thing about the room, Marlayna decided, was that it was quiet and cool and devoid of a king. Her eyes rolled in mute appeal. Arthur Kingman hadn't been easy to dislodge. For a while, she really had expected the man to escort her through every room in the castle and then aid her in unpacking.

She had dutifully listened to the history behind this tapestry and the cost of that antique, the number of craftsmen that had been hired to duplicate the hand-carved woodwork and of artisans that had painstakingly blown the crystal for the chandeliers, and all the rest of it until she could have screamed.

"But, of course, you didn't." Marlayna spoke her congratulatory words out loud. "You nodded and smiled and ohhed and ahhed in all the right spots and at the proper time. Arthur was so impressed." She twisted her nose and mouth in an exaggerated manner.

Her savior had been the telephone and a call from a reporter on *Architectural Digest*. "I shall buy a subscription as a thank-you," Marlayna vowed. The phone conversation promised to be lengthy, and she used that well-timed distraction to escape from Arthur and retire to her room. Here, lying quietly on the bed, Marlayna thought about the man she had seen in the elevator.

He was her Noah Drake, all right. Marlayna closed her eyes and instantly he appeared. His hair was as thick and dark as it was a half dozen years ago. The planes and angles of his face were more pronounced; the shape leaner, harsher; the complexion bronzed by the sun; and that old nemesis of a five o'clock shadow still very much in evidence on his cheeks and square jaw.

Perhaps the most shocking change was in Noah's posture and his obvious dependency on a cane. *Cane.* That black curve of metal seemed part of his anatomy, like an extra leg. Trembling fingers rubbed across Marlayna's forehead as she remembered his body.

Despite a slight roundness, Noah's shoulders were as broad and looked even stronger than they had when he worked in construction. His torso was better developed, the sinewy muscles exposed by the half-lowered zipper on his jacket. It was his legs that became magnified in her mind. The large scars that streaked his flesh were quite vivid despite the dark curly hairs that matted his skin.

Marlayna knew what her fate had been, but now she wondered about Noah's. From all appearances,

Fate had not been kind. Had all the unkindness changed the inner man? How ironic that she was now in a profession that glorified outward perfection and beauty. And yet, none of that mattered to her; it had never mattered.

Despite her concern, Marlayna couldn't help but smile as she remembered the expression on Noah's face just as the elevator door snapped shut. "Dumbfounded." An airy giggle punctured the quiet. It was an expression that she had seen on his face only once before—the first time they met.

The emergency room at Grady Memorial Hospital in Atlanta had been the scene of that auspicious occasion. Her grin drooped as she remembered that the same room was also the scene for their last meeting. Resolutely Marlayna pushed away the last memory and concentrated on the first.

Eyes closed, her mind effortlessly replayed another scene from the past. That Wednesday morning in ER had looked exactly like a beehive gone berserk. Driving winds and rain had caused a ten-car pile-up on one of the city's main traffic arteries with over thirty people in need of and demanding various medical services.

Marlayna's job as admissions/insurance clerk rated way above average on the verbal abuse scale, slightly higher even than the blood technician who answered to "Dracula." She had become quite proficient in answering those who clutched random parts of their anatomy while moaning, "I'm dying and she wants my Blue Cross/Blue Shield number!"

On that particular day, during the waning hours of bedlam, another patient arrived. A dark-haired, dark-eyed construction worker, his left arm swathed in bloody handkerchiefs, somehow managed to circumvent the indomitable Miss O'Brian and ended up in a treatment room before filling out the proper forms. After discovering the infraction Marlayna fearlessly charged into the white-curtained cubicle.

Her first view of the patient made her face turn scarlet; she found herself gazing at his bare bottom! "Excuse me——"

"Well, I'm all ready for you, nurse," his deep voice interrupted as he continued to inspect his newly bandaged arm from his prone position on a gurney. "Those automatic staple guns certainly have a mind of their own at times. That doctor did a nice job getting those four brads out."

Receiving nothing but a guttural acknowledgment, he turned his head. "Say, can you hurry this penicillin shot up; I've got to get back and——" His brown eyes suddenly narrowed. "You're not the nurse who was just in here."

Her wide-eyed inspection of his well-muscled buttocks was interrupted when she shook her head and tapped her name badge with a pen. "I'm not a nurse; I'm the admissions clerk."

"Not . . . a . . . nurse . . ." His puckered forehead lifted and smoothed with that discovery. "Jeezus . . . lady!" His right arm jerked backward, hand groping for a white sheet that was yanked to his waist. "Don't you treat your patients with dignity in this joint? Since when am I a peep show!"

She took a deep breath and moved to stand in front of him. "I've seen better peep shows," Marlayna lied coolly. "Now, let's get you registered as a patient and then I'll be glad to leave you and your dignity in the hands of the nursing staff."

With her pencil poised over the clipboarded forms, she rapidly fired questions at him: "Name, address and phone?"

"Noah Drake; eighty-nine Collins Street, apartment two-oh-three; five, five, five, ninety-one, seventy."

"Age, doctor and employer?"

"Twenty-nine; Dr. Harper; Caldour Construction."

"Medical insurance, the company and your group and individual number?"

Coming up on his good right elbow, Noah flung his bandaged left arm out for her inspection. "Listen, lady! I just had four two-inch-long staples removed from this wrist, which, I might add, aches like hell, and what do I get? Questions!" He shook his head and shot a disgusted look at her. "Where's your compassion? Where's your sympathy? Where's your——"

"Insurance card," came her no-nonsense reply. Marlayna gave him a sweet smile. "I've heard it all before, Mr. Drake. Come on, the card? I don't have all day."

"It's in the back pocket of my jeans." His thumb jerked toward the pants that were, along with his white briefs, draped across a nearby chair.

"May I?"

Noah's lips twisted in a sarcastic smile. "Be my guest. What's a pocket between us? After all, you've already seen what's *in* the pants."

Marlayna could feel his eyes gauge her every movement, and when she bent over to retrieve his wallet, his low wolf whistle again caused her color to come up. "That was really quite unnecessary, Mr. Drake."

"What can I say?" He gave her his best grin. "I'm a man who appreciates a well-curved female, although

I'd really love to appreciate that cute rear end of yours in the same condition that you appreciated mine."

She continued to copy the long string of numbers that was on his insurance card. "Many men have tried, Mr. Drake."

"And I get the feeling they have all failed."

Marlayna snapped the wallet closed and dropped it on top of his pants. "Could I have your signature at the x's, please?" She balanced the clipboard on the edge of the gurney and handed him her pen.

He peered at her left breast. "Yes, Miss O'Brian," and scrawled his name in the three spots. "What time do you get off work?"

"Six o'clock. Why?"

Noah wagged the pen between his thumb and index finger. "I'd like to continue appreciating you over dinner for your service above and beyond the call of duty."

She plucked the pen free just as the nurse returned to the room with a tray that contained a very large needle. Marlayna squatted down so that guileless blue gray eyes were on level with his láughing brown ones. "I just may let you, Mr. Drake. Somehow, I think I'll be perfectly safe with a one-armed, sore-fannied man." Her wink came just seconds before his inhaled shriek of pain.

A double knock on the door of the suite abruptly invaded Marlayna's dream and brought her to a sitting position. "Yes?" No answer, but the knock was repeated more sharply. "Yes?" she called out loudly, but again no response. "Well, I suppose a room with walls of granite and a wooden door two feet thick is relatively soundproof!"

She wriggled off the bed and straightened her

clothes as she walked to the door, hoping that the caller wouldn't be Arthur Kingman.

It wasn't. The instant she opened the door, Noah Drake stepped inside. Her blue gray eyes meshed with warm brown ones, and all her dreams and longings suddenly interlaced with her life.

"It is you." His cane thudded against the carpet as shaking hands cupped her face. "I wasn't sure." He visually worshiped every feature. "I'm still not."

His left palm was warm against her cheek, his fingers held captive by ebony curls. Ever so slowly, his right hand began to move. Five trembling fingers caressed her skin, reveling in the velvety softness of her complexion, moving along the curve of her brow and ruffling the delicate sweep of dark lashes.

"I didn't believe it." Noah's voice was hoarse, strained and unsure. His thumbs tenderly defined her cheekbones and slid down to her chin before settling on either side of her mouth. "I . . . I . . . am I dreaming?"

Questioning his sanity, Noah mapped the slender sweep of her neck and pressed hard through the thin silk of her blouse into her upper arms. His senses reeled with the exhilarating discovery that she did, indeed, exist and was right here. "Mimi?"

Her eyes were riveted on his. "Yes, Noah."

"Thank God." His whispered words of gratitude caught her off guard; so did his tears and his kiss.

It seemed an eternity before his lips made that most vital connection. His head turned and twisted as it drew closer to hers, so frantic was he to make this first kiss say so much. But the instant his lips touched hers, anxiety gave way to sheer bliss. And for the first time in six years, Noah Drake felt alive.

His kiss was everything Marlayna remembered—and more. His mouth was warm and wonderfully soft and sweet as it found hers. She reached up and caressed the stubbled curve of his jaw with her knuckles. "Oh, Noah . . ."

But his aggressive mouth consumed the rest of her words. This kiss was alternately tender and dominating as Noah's arms bonded her trembling body tightly against his. Her hands traveled up his jacketed arms, slithered across his shoulders to let her fingers filter through the dark hair that hugged his nape. The thick strands moved like silk against her skin, the fresh clean scent of him drugging her senses.

She gave up trying to think and let herself be swept away by the sheer sorcery of his touch. His tongue gently trespassed into the inviting depths of her mouth, savoring the honeyed sweetness as his own life-giving nectar.

With a low moan, Marlayna pulled her mouth free and brushed away her tears and then his with gentle fingertips. "I'm not sure why I'm kissing you, Noah Drake." Her tremulous voice tried to sound angry.

"Because you still love me."

"That's not good enough."

"Because I've always loved you."

Her hands fell away from his shoulders to settle on her hips. "Is that why you divorced me? Is that why you're engaged to another woman?" Her words sounded sharper, harder. "Are you in love with Gwen Kingman?"

Noah's fingers bit tightly into the curve of her waist. "Yes. I'm not. No."

She blinked and repeated his answer, stuttering all the way. Marlayna cleared her throat and tried to be coherent. "I'd like a clarification, Mr. Drake."

He hauled her closer. "And I'd like more kisses at the very least, Mrs. Drake."

"*Miss* O'Brian," came her caustic correction. "Your lawyer said you had insisted."

A shadow crossed his face and dulled his eyes. "I did what I had to, Mimi. I never thought I'd be standing and holding you ever again."

His enunciation of that word *standing* caused her immediate concern. "Noah, would you like to sit down and——"

"Nope." He tilted her chin up. "This is what I'd like to do." Again and again, he kissed her. Quick, hard kisses. Lingering, gentle ones. He placed light butterfly kisses on each closed eyelid, another on the tip of her nose and the small indentation in her chin.

Noah's lips traveled along the sensitive cord on her neck. "You still wear the same perfume, the one that always made me a little crazy," he murmured huskily. He liberated her blouse from the waistband of her white slacks and slid his hands warmly over her back. "You feel so good, taste so good . . ."

She was getting ready to make another staunch protest, but his insistent mouth and tongue robbed her of all rational thought. It's not really fair, Marlayna thought. He's always been able to set me on fire. But when she felt Noah shudder in her arms, she knew that she had the same power over him.

Then she felt his hand move from her spine to her breast, his skillful fingers trying to free the taut nipple from its lacy prison. "Noah!" Marlayna wriggled from his grasp as she felt his body harden beneath the thin covering of his swim trunks. "You are an engaged man."

His lips twisted. "I suppose you want to talk about all this right now."

"I want to know *everything*—then and now."

He ran a shaky hand through his hair. "I guess we had better sit down. Could you hand me my cane?"

"Do you always need it?"

"Right now"—Noah slipped his left arm around her waist as they walked to the pink-cushioned loveseat— "I *feel* as if I could pick you up and carry you to that bed. But I can't. I never will. Does that bother you?"

Marlayna snuggled into the curve of his body, her head resting on his shoulder, his fingers entwined with hers. "No. As I recall, you never did pick me up and carry me any place."

"I did too!" he returned defensively. "Right across the threshold of our house when we got back from the honeymoon."

"Oh, yeah." Then she whispered in his ear, "But you complained about the ache in your back for three days."

"That back ache wasn't from lifting you." His grin vanished. "And I wish my back and legs would ache for only three days now."

She bit her lip. "How bad is it?"

"Some days like hell." Noah was quiet for a long moment; he pressed his lips against her forehead. "How much did you learn about my accident?"

"Nothing. Nobody would even talk to me. I was crazy with worry and all I got was——"

"You got exactly what we decided to give you. Nothing."

Her free hand spread across his bare thigh, her fingernail tracing the wide scar that seemed to have no end. "I want all the answers now." Marlayna stared into his eyes. "First and most important, are you in love with Gwen?"

He shook his head.

"Then why are we all here celebrating your engagement?"

"She's engaged to me. I'm not engaged to her."

"You're not making any sense, Noah."

His lips curved. "I know. I know. God, it's so damn complicated. I'm not sure this *engagement* can be explained."

"You better try." Marlayna sat up straight against the cushions, arms crossed over her chest, and waited.

Noah rubbed the tension from the back of his neck. "As near as I can remember, it happened about ten weeks ago. Gwen was here, helping finalize the decorating while I was redesigning that damn boat house. We were talking and drinking and . . ." He swallowed and coughed. "And she asked me and . . . and I guess . . . I must have said yes."

"You guess?"

"Hell, I don't remember."

Marlayna looked skeptical. "How long have you known her?"

"Three and half months."

"Ever kiss her?"

"No." His response was quick. "I wouldn't even have given her a second glance, except she reminded me of you."

"Oh, Noah, that's sweet." Her soft tone was transformed into an interrogatory one. "Why would two people who never even kissed get engaged?"

His head lowered, chin pressed into his chest. "She's . . . she's in love with me. Built a fantasy out of every kind word I've ever said and has convinced herself that one-sided love is better than no love at all."

"Hmmm . . . well, I know Arthur is thrilled to pieces over having you as a son-in-law."

"Yeah, there's that too," Noah agreed. "The man's been good to me. Met me through an employee of his that I was designing a house for and hired me to revamp this charming little castle. Arthur Kingman's a powerful man and—" He stopped and looked at Marlayna. "Say, how the hell do you know Arthur? And what are you doing here anyway?"

"You mean you don't know about me and Arthur?"

"You and Arthur?" he echoed in rage. "You and Arthur!"

Marlayna stood up. "Now . . . it's not like that. Although Arthur sort of wishes it were." As anger further contorted Noah's face, she hastened to explain: "Listen, I'm his——" Her answer was interrupted by a knock on the door. Blue eyes locked into brown. "You don't suppose that's him ?"

"At your *bedroom* door?"

"Don't make it sound like 'mission impossible,'" came her haughty rejoinder. "Quite a few men would have liked to pound on my bedroom door over the past six years, mister!" Marlayna drew herself up and calmly walked to the door. She situated herself so that her body blocked the rest of the room from view. "Yes?"

"Excuse me, miss, I'm Perkins, the household manager. I'm looking for Mr. Drake."

Her expression was insouciant. "And whatever makes you think he's here?"

"Because Perkins told me where you were," Noah answered. "Let him in, Mimi." Reaching for his cane, he struggled off the sofa. "What's up, Perkins?"

"Both Miss Gwen and Mr. Kingman are looking for

you, sir." He took an antique watch from the pocket of his vest and snapped it open. "The guests are beginning to mingle on the terrace for the cocktail party."

Marlayna gasped. "Oh, damn! I haven't even started to get ready."

"You never did tell me why you're here," Noah persisted.

"I'm Arthur's 'Face of the Century.'" At his confused expression, she walked to the dresser and got the new issue of *Vogue*. "For his cosmetic empire." She pointed to her photograph on the cover. "See."

Noah did a double take. "That's not you." He grabbed the magazine and showed it to Perkins. "Is that her?"

The manager looked down his rather prominent nose and replied: "I do believe it is, sir." His blue gaze studied Marlayna's face. "A stunning cover, miss."

"Thank you, Perkins." She gave him a smile before turning to Noah. "I've been extolling the magic of Kingman Cosmetics for the last year, and their sales have doubled."

"I don't believe it."

"Well, thanks a lot," Marlayna returned huffily. "This face"—she tapped her cheek—"has made me a small fortune. Arthur Kingman happens to love this face and the rest of me as well," came her nasty addendum.

"And has he had a chance to?" Noah asked, in an equally nasty tone.

"Sir." Perkins again tapped his watch. "The time. Miss, the party."

"All right. All right," Noah snapped. "I'm going to want a few answers later myself, Mimi."

"Not as many as I want, Noah Drake." She turned and with a slam of the door, disappeared into the adjoining bathroom.

Walking down the castle's wide granite-walled hallway, Noah finally broke the silence. "Uh, Perkins, I know what you must be thinking——"

"I'm not paid to think, sir."

His hand reached for the butler's arm. "Stop a minute, will you." Noah looked up the extra four inches past his own six-foot height that was needed to stare into the man's blue eyes. "Now, Perkins, how long have we known each other?"

"Going on nearly two years, sir."

"And in that time, when it was just you and me and the work crew on the island, how much money have you beaten me out of at cribbage?"

"Quite a bit, sir."

"Enough to make you think?"

Perkins allowed a brief laugh to escape his closed lips; his expression, however, remained stoic. "I think, sir, that while you're dressing for the party, I'll bring you that triple scotch and perhaps pour a double for myself and then we can think about all this together."

"Brilliant, Perkins." Noah sighed. "You always know the proper thing to do."

5

·ooooooooooo·

Twisting the hot faucet off and holding her breath, Marlayna waited for the cold water to hit. The icy wash needled into her back and across her shoulders, invigorating her physically and energizing her mentally. She counted to ten, quickly ended the shower, wrapped her shivering form in a fluffy rose bath towel and stepped out of the cubicle onto the white tiled floor of a bathroom that was the size of most people's living room.

Bathroom, she decided with an irreverent grin, was such a bourgeois word to call this impressive ensemble of intimate furnishings. The room continued the bedroom suite's pastel pink theme, with sink, toilet, tub and bidet all blushing against white Roman tiles. A crystal chandelier shimmered over a sunken tub surrounded by a garden of potted palms and ten parakeets that were artificial but had eyes that stared with unsettling interest.

Marlayna found herself duplicated into infinity in the floor-to-ceiling mirrors that paneled two of the walls. "Nice." She patted her cheek and in doing so patted hundreds of others. "But we don't have time for more than the original right now." With a silent promise to wallow in bubbles for at least an hour in the Jacuzzi tub, she adjourned to the globe-lit mirror over the pedestal sink and began to make up the "Face of the Century."

"So, Noah Drake, you had trouble believing this face could grace a magazine cover, did you?" She leaned closer to the mirror and inspected the insulted area. "Well, granted, it's not a remarkable face. In fact, it's a pretty ordinary face." Marlayna picked up the bottle of foundation and a tiny cosmetic sponge. "Canvas. That's what the makeup men always call a face—a canvas on which to create a masterpiece of color and shadows and illusion."

She found her *canvas* needed very little in the way of artificial enhancement. The seemingly interminable malaise that had been her companion for so many years had ended. Now every part of her bloomed. Her movements were more graceful, her hair a shiny pelt of sable curls; her eyes shone brilliant as lapis lazuli gemstones, and her complexion radiated the inner excitement that was making her feel quite intoxicated.

This was the same giddiness that had always assaulted her senses when she first started dating Noah—a delicious rainbow of emotions that made her feel brand new and on the verge of experiencing something wonderful. Marlayna twisted the cap on the tube of navy mascara closed and reached for her brush to shape and fluff her hair. Her hand hovered for a moment before closing tightly around the wooden handle.

"Damn Noah!" With that sudden explosion, her expression changed. "He got away without explaining one darn thing. The man even had the gall to make a few snide insinuations."

Marlayna inhaled deeply. "I'm insulted. He expects a few kisses to wipe out all the agony." The brush's wide bristles whipped her curls into an elegant disarray. "That man is arrogant, nervy and too damn sure of himself and me. No woman likes to be taken for granted, especially when she hasn't been *taken* for anything in the last six years."

By the time a slip dress of red satin Charmeuse replaced the terry bath towel and stockings and high-heeled evening sandals graced her legs and feet, Marlayna still hadn't any idea of what she was going to say or do or how she was going to act not only toward Noah but toward Arthur Kingman and daughter Gwen.

Her two index fingers coaxed fiery lips upward. "Well, at least you look and feel terrific, lady." With a flirty wink at her reflection and a devil-may-care smile on her face, she left to join the party.

King Arthur headed a receiving line of three. He kissed her hand and inspected her from toe to head. His gray eyes scrutinized her face for a long moment before a plethora of compliments erupted. "I've exhausted the dictionary and still there is no word that could describe such loveliness, such exquisite beauty."

Normally, Marlayna would have given him one of her well-rehearsed professional smiles while she slithered her hand from his, but not tonight. Tonight, her ego needed the attention, the fawning and the flattery. In fact her mood matched the weather: sultry.

So she let him kiss her hand a second time and

decided to repay his appreciation in kind. "Arthur, you are the perfect host. There isn't a thing to want."

He leaned closer to her and said in a low whisper, "There is *one* thing that I want, that only *you* can give, Marlayna——"

She giggled girlishly, interrupting what she knew was a very personal *want*. Her kohl-rimmed eyes slanted to his left. "And this must be your Gwen."

Arthur cleared his throat, adjusted his black bowtie and then smoothed the lapels on his white evening jacket. "Yes. Darling, this is Marlayna O'Brian, she's——"

"Why, Daddy, I know who she is. I do look at our advertising." Gwen extended her hand and smiled. "It's a pleasure to finally see you other than on the pages of a magazine, Miss O'Brian."

"Please, make it Marlayna." Her gaze drifted toward the man who stood next to Gwen, a man who was staring at her with yet another dumbfounded expression on his face. She decided to anticipate Arthur's introduction, simply because she didn't want to hear that Noah was Gwen's fiancé. "And this must be Noah Drake, the architect you were telling me about earlier, Arthur." Both her hands encompassed his. "The castle is incredible."

"Thank you," came his dry acknowledgment.

"Marlayna." Arthur moved quickly to her side, his hand curving in a proprietary gesture around her bare upper arm. "Let me get you a drink and introduce you to my other guests." His fingers rubbed against silken skin. "I want everyone to have the pleasure of meeting you."

Her eyes were focused on Noah's face; he looked ready to explode. And that made her feel even more reckless and daring. This seemed the perfect time to flirt and enjoy and be carried along with events. After all, she was a sophisticated, mature woman. A *single* woman, who hadn't had any fun in six years. Marlayna favored her host with a beaming smile. "That's terribly sweet, Arthur. I'd be honored."

Noah took a step to halt Marlayna's progress but found his own impeded when the rubber tip of his cane became tangled in the lace on Gwen's long gown. "Oops. Sorry."

Inhaling sharply, she hastily straightened the halter neckline and then reeled up a yard of the fragile material for inspection. "Nothing ripped." Gwen looked from the dress to her father. "I think Miss O'Brian may become a permanent acquisition of Daddy's."

"What's that supposed to mean?"

Her brow arched at the roughness in his voice. "It means that Daddy likes her. I can always tell, he gets this glazed look and——"

"And what?"

Gwen gave a little shrug. "What Daddy likes and wants, he always manages to get." She twisted her head slightly to look at him. "We both share that trait."

He shifted more of his weight onto the cane. "That might work for *things*, Gwen, but not for people."

She bit her lip. "Especially not for you?" When he made no reply, her hand curled around the cuff of his dinner jacket. "You've ignored me for most of the day." Her lower lip pouted. "And why did you tell Daddy not to make any sort of announcement about our engagement? It was printed on the invitations. I feel humiliated."

"I wasn't consulted about the invitations. In fact, I wasn't even consulted about the engagement." Noah took a deep breath and altered the harsh tone of his voice. "Look, there's that tennis player with the unpronounceable name. Why don't you go get some pointers."

Her brown eyes lit up. "Come with me and—"

"I think in my case it would be rather pointless."

"I . . . I'm sorry. I . . . just . . . didn't think."

Noah's smile was kind. "At your age you shouldn't have to think about things like that." He put his hand against the small of her back and gave her a little shove. "Go on. We'll talk later."

"Tact and diplomacy. Tact and diplomacy." Noah repeatedly mumbled that phrase as he nodded and smiled and skirted his way around the nearly two hundred people who were enjoying drinks and appetizers on the massive walled terrace.

Yes, tact, diplomacy with a healthy topping of delicacy. Those would be the perfect ingredients needed to edge out of this one-sided engagement and still maintain some sort of friendly relationship with Arthur Kingman. Odd, a dozen years ago he would have been more forthright, perhaps even brutal, about setting this situation straight. But with a man as powerful as King Arthur, a man known for taking great pleasure in the ruination of an enemy, honesty and the direct approach was not the way to go.

Stopping to rest, Noah let his gaze wander over the crowd. He quickly focused on one laughing, chattering woman. A woman surrounded by an attentive conclave of men. A woman clad in a rather scandalous siren-red dress. A woman he still considered his wife.

She was not behaving at all like *his* Mimi. She didn't

even look like *his* Mimi. Noah settled on an out-of-the-way pink marble patio bench that was shielded from view by a topiary garden of miniature evergreens pruned to resemble chess pieces. Peering through a rook, he began to dissect her. He decided to start at the top with her hair.

Perkins interrupted his musings by inquiring whether he needed anything. "Yes. You." Noah patted the polished bench top. "Have a seat, Perkins; I need your opinion."

"Really, sir, I'm a bit busy at the moment with the *other* guests. When I saw you ambling to this spot to rest, I thought perhaps you could use this scotch." He extended a silver tray. "Perhaps these shrimp puffs would substitute."

Noah pulled him down despite his continued blustery refusal. "Nonsense, you deserve a break. No one can see us. I'll take this." He confiscated the glass. "You munch on the shrimp puffs." A healthy mouthful of liquor fueled him on to attack his subject. "What do you think of Miss O'Brian's hair?"

Perkins's gray brows lifted. "Her hair, sir?"

"Yes. You know, this is the first time I've seen her with it short. She always wore her hair long." His voice was dreamy. "Brushed back from her forehead and whispering against her shoulders. It felt like silk, Perkins. Midnight silk."

Clearing his throat, Noah continued. "Now . . . well . . . hmmm . . ." He pushed a branch to one side, his gaze narrowing on Marlayna. "I do like the way those little wisps curl around her ears. She's got great ears, Perkins. And her nape is exposed. A lovely sweep. And, you know the way it tumbles onto her forehead . . . well . . . that is kind of"—a deep chuckle rumbled in his chest—"sexy in a tumbled, rumpled, wild sort of way."

The butler merely grunted as he bit into a slice of cucumber topped with red caviar, crumbled egg and a black olive.

"I suppose she has to wear all that makeup because she's Arthur's 'Face of the Century.'" He looked at his companion. "Rather a gutsy statement, don't you think?"

"She doesn't seem to be snobbish about it, sir." Perkins returned carefully. "As a matter of fact, I'd say Miss O'Brian was wearing much less in the way of paint than the other ladies in attendance."

Noah looked around and made a guttural sound of agreement. "You're right. I guess I'm not used to seeing her looking like this. You know, when we were married our schedules were too damn different. Sometimes we went for days without seeing each other. She'd work nights and go to school days; I'd work days and go to school at night.

"I remember her face all soft and pink from sleep, and when she went to work, she used only a little lipstick and a dab of powder. And perfume." He took a deep breath, becoming drugged by an imaginary scent that rivaled the fragrant flowers that flanked the patio. "I've never forgotten her perfume, Perkins. She still wears the same one."

"My mother always drenched herself in lilac water." The house manager sighed. His finger squeezed the nostrils on his large nose. "To this day I still feel surrounded by that odious smell."

"But I bet your mother never wore a dress like that." Noah reached for a cream-cheese-stuffed cherry tomato. "That thing is positively indecent. Look at it. No, don't." His back molars pulverized the fragile canape. "I don't know how much longer those skinny little straps can hold up that . . . that . . . thin slice of silk."

His eyes darkened as they took in the dropped waistline and scalloped hem that danced against Marlayna's knees. "She never owned anything like that. All her dresses were high-necked, long-sleeved, mid-calf. Nothing with that type of neckline."

Plunging. If he could see the creamy swells of her breasts, so could every man in the room. And even worse, if he stared hard enough, he saw that her nipples pushed brazenly against the slinky, slippery bodice. With each move she made, the sinuous fabric shimmered and delineated every lush curve on her body.

Noah shifted in discomfort and quickly downed the last of the scotch. "I don't remember her having a body quite like that either, Perkins. She was never that . . . that . . ."

"Sexy, sir?"

"Yeah. Sexy. She was more wifely. Homey. Old-fashioned."

"Well, sir, it seems that saying, 'Women don't get older, they get better,' is quite true in Miss O'Brian's case."

He grunted. "Well, I always thought she was better. The best. Why else would I have married her?"

Perkins ran a hand through the thin sweep of gray hair that covered his head. "I've been in service to a number of married couples, sir. And I've discovered there are lots of reasons for people marrying."

"Like what?" He looked at him with interest.

"Money, power, loneliness, revenge, spite."

Noah shook his head. "Sounds more like the ingredients of a TV soap opera."

"Life does have a way of imitating and often surpassing art, sir."

"Well, I married that"—his index finger jabbed into the bush—"woman for love. That's the same reason I divorced her. And the same reason I intend to marry her all over again."

Perkins looked at Noah, his face devoid of any expression. "Even with all the changes in her?"

"I don't really mind all her changes." His expression turned bleak. "But I wonder how she likes all of mine." Noah stared morosely at the ice cubes that were melting in his glass.

"The cane, sir?"

"Yeah. My little partner here." He patted the black wood. "I do like this better than that wheelchair."

"What has been Miss O'Brian's reaction to it?" Perkins inquired in an even voice.

"Interest, of course. I've yet to tell her about everything." Noah sighed and ran a hand over his face. "But at least she doesn't seem to pity me. I couldn't handle that, Perkins. Gwen does, and it annoys the hell out of me."

Perkins cleared his throat. "About Miss Gwen, sir?"

"Oh, God, I've got to handle her and Arthur just right. You know how he can be."

"Indeed I do, sir."

Noah spread open another branch to inspect the gathering. "Look at her, Perkins. Mimi fits right into this crowd. She's undaunted by the politicians, plays kissy-kissy with the Hollywood group, shares intimate little mutterings with the jet-setters. Makes me wonder . . ."

"About what, sir?" Perkins inspected the last shrimp puff carefully before placing it into his mouth.

"She always hated parties. She was shy and hesitant. And here she is making cutesy with everyone." Noah turned his head. "Do you know she once volunteered to work a double shift because she didn't want to attend the hospital Christmas party and couldn't come up with a good excuse."

Noah took a deep breath. "I guess the thing that really bothers me is her obvious fame. It's hard for me to imagine my wife gracing the covers of magazines or her eye makeup being copied by millions of women across America. Kind of shattering to a man's ego, wouldn't you say, Perkins?"

"I'd be rather proud of Miss O'Brian, if it were I, sir. She obviously is quite adept at handling people and situations, and she seems to take her fame with a modicum of humility. There are other women present, a few of them models, starlets, and wives of various important men, who flaunt their status and success ad nauseam. I see none of that coming from Miss O'Brian."

"Why thank you, Perkins," a cheery feminine voice interrupted. "That was a lovely thing to say."

"You're quite welcome, miss." Perkins adjusted the cuffs on his formal serving jacket before standing up. "May I bring you something?"

Marlayna lifted her champagne glass. "No thanks. I just thought I'd come over here and toast Casanova."

Noah snickered.

"Now . . . now . . . take that look out of your eye, Mr. Drake." She sat in the reverse direction on the seat Perkins had just vacated. "I saw the way Gwen fairly sparkles when she looks at you." Marlayna rubbed the crystal goblet against his jaw. "Of course, I can't blame her; you're especially devastating tonight in this formal white suit."

"It seems *you* have a rather devastating effect on Arthur," came his snarling comment. "Of course, it could be that dress."

"This little old thing." Her voice was high and innocent. "Why I just threw it on."

"Little is right and you could have aimed better." Noah turned his head. "Don't you realize the way every man here can see your body?"

"How insulting! I've spent the last six years worried and agonizing over you and now you have the nerve to attack my morals."

"Not your morals," he shot back, "only your cleavage!"

She sipped her wine and thought about it for a moment. "I always thought you liked my cleavage." Marlayna looked down at her breasts. "If I remember correctly, you never saw the last reel of *Gone With the Wind* because you were terribly involved in exploring my cleavage."

He tried to stop the grin that was forming but failed. "Atlanta wasn't the only thing burning that night. We really steamed up the windows in that Maverick. And you're right"—the fingers on his right hand walked up her arm and down between the valley of her breasts— "I love your cleavage."

The satin swells burgeoned under his fingertips, the nipples thrusting aggressively against the thin dress covering them. Noah leaned even closer, his warm breath caressing her ear. "It's been an awful long time since I made love to you any place but in my dreams."

Marlayna lifted his hand clear of her breast. "So you think we can just pick up where we left off? Just like that?" Her eyes were more ice gray than blue. "I haven't even had the decency of an explanation about"—she waved her hand—"anything. And then of course there's Gwen."

Noah groaned. "How like a woman to mention another woman."

"It seems I'm the *other* woman in this affair."

"There is no affair, if that's what you're worried about." His finger eased between his shirt collar and neck, trying to gain more comfort. "I . . . I just need a little time. Handling Gwen and Arthur is going to require a lot of tact and diplomacy."

She brushed an imaginary speck off her skirt while she digested that comment. "*They* require tact and diplomacy. And what about me? Am I supposed to jump into your arms and into your bed just like"—she snapped her fingers—"that?"

"I love you. You love me. That should be enough." His voice grew husky as his knuckles caressed her jaw. "It was the first time."

"I'm not sure you ever did love me."

"I loved you enough not to hurt you." He cupped her chin and turned her face toward his. "I couldn't hurt you, Mimi. I'd sooner walk away——"

"That's just what you did, Noah."

"No, that's just the point. I couldn't."

Her forehead puckered. "Couldn't what?"

"Couldn't walk. The doctors told me I'd never walk."

"You're giving a pretty fair imitation of it right now."

Noah's inflection changed from a sorrowful calm to a low-toned rage. "That's because for the last five years I've undergone countless operations, been a guinea pig for all sorts of medical experiments, had every kind of therapy imaginable and am the proud owner of legs that cost over a million dollars! You keep mentioning agony. Lady, you don't know what agony is!"

"Oh, don't I?" Marlayna's voice was as deadly as his. "How dare you—?"

"I dare because I've been sitting here watching you, Miss 'Face of the Century.'" He spat the words as though they soured his mouth. "By the looks of things you haven't been pining away."

"Well, looks can be deceiving."

"Really? You seem to be on kissing terms with every Tom, Dick and Arthur here!"

Marlayna lunged to her feet. "I'd like to take that cane and bash it over your head." Her eyes were glittering slits. "You may have six-million-dollar legs, Noah Drake, but your brain isn't worth two cents! I don't think I'd wish you on any woman, not even Gwen Kingman."

Noah made a grab for her arm. "Where do you think you're going?"

She effortlessly moved out of his reach. "Back to the party. Back to give every Tom, Dick and Arthur another kiss."

"Wait a minute. Don't you dare walk away from me." He grabbed his cane and struggled to a standing position. "I love you, damn it."

Marlayna lifted her shoulders in a carefree shrug. "Really? Well, you're certainly making a lousy effort to convince me."

"Just what in hell is that supposed to mean?"

She inspected her manicure before speaking. "I'm not quite sure."

His harassed, confused expression matched hers. "If you don't know what you want, how am I supposed to know?" Noah sat back on the bench and waited.

The dinner gong turned out to be her savior. "Maybe I'll think of something while we're enjoying Arthur's kingly feast." Without a backward glance Marlayna blithely strolled in to mingle with the others who were exchanging the terrace garden for the banquet hall.

If she hadn't seen it with her own eyes and actually been a part of it, Marlayna would have claimed that it was impossible to serve two hundred people a sit-down dinner all at the same time. But the vaulted ceilings in the castle's massive dining room echoed with applause once everyone took their assigned seats at the tables, which were arranged in the shape of a horseshoe.

Her seat was on the inside curve. On her left was the senior senator from New York, on her right a movie producer from Hollywood, immediately across was an ambassador and his wife. Catty-cornered was Arthur's smiling face; on the left and farther down, Noah's scowling one.

Shaking out a red linen napkin emblazoned with the Kingman crest, Marlayna knew the next move with Noah was up to her. "And for the life of me, I don't know what to do!" she mumbled to herself. "Or exactly what I want," she added ruefully.

No, that wasn't quite true. Marlayna knew what she wanted. She wanted to be away from all these people; away from all the gossip and laughter. She wanted to be with Noah in a secluded spot so they could talk and share their respective agonies and see if their future was to be together.

"More champagne, miss?"

"Thank you, Perkins." She smiled at his intense expression. "Everything looks wonderful. I don't know how you and the staff managed all this."

"Neither do I." His eyes glanced left and right. "Henry the Eighth never hosted such a gathering." Perkins wiped the neck of the bottle of Moët with a white cloth. "If I may say, Miss O'Brian, Mr. Drake is a bit overwhelmed by your status."

Marlayna leaned back into the red leather chair so she could speak without her table companions listening. "What would you suggest I do?"

He was thoughtful a moment while his fingers deftly rearranged two forks that were in reverse order. "Men, unfortunately, have quite fragile egos, miss." Perkins gave her a minuscule little bow and moved on to fill the next empty goblet.

So that was it! Noah was having an ego problem. Marlayna slanted a casual glance in his direction and found that he was staring at her. She hastily looked away. A deflated ego was a bit out of character for him. Not that he had ever been a swaggering Mr. Macho. But Noah had always been a very self-confident man, sure of himself in any situation.

Maybe she had overwhelmed him. He kept commenting on her appearance and pointing to his own. Yes, Noah's disability was one that could be seen. But she had one too—a disability that had affected her heart, mind and soul.

Suddenly, it came to her just what her next step should be. Marlayna had to reinforce Noah's own knowledge that he was a desirable man, that she was attracted to him, that she wanted him. "I certainly do," she whispered as she lifted the water goblet to her mouth.

Arthur Kingman's deep voice invaded her private deliberations. Marlayna cheered and lifted her glass in the air along with one hundred ninety-nine others, but she wasn't listening to a word the man was saying. Another man occupied a more important place in her mind.

She decided to employ that age-old technique of feminine warfare—flirting, or, as the French called it, *faire les yeux doux*, to make sweet eyes. Again, Marlayna turned toward Noah and, as before, found that he was watching her.

This time she didn't look away. She stared at him as if he were the only man in the room while letting her lips curve in a subtle smile. His gaze narrowed, then widened, his brown eyes sending back a speculative inquiry. She fluttered her lashes, then lowered her eyes, pretending great interest in the vichyssoise that was served.

She managed to send playful, encouraging little glances at Noah while eating classic English mutton chops, an endive and watercress salad with basil dressing and Dungeness crab with mustard sauce.

Furthermore, she handled all that flirting without being rude to her immediate companions, although one coquettish flutter did go off its mark and fall onto Arthur Kingman, who responded with a wink of his own. "Hmmm . . ." She blotted her mouth with her napkin. "I think I'd better find someone to waylay the king of this castle," she murmured as she proceeded to inspect the other women in attendance.

Perkins politely announced his presence by clearing his throat next to Noah's ear. "How is everything, sir?"

"Looking more promising with every course. You

know, Perkins, I don't think I'll ever understand that woman. She keeps saying 'no,' but those eyes and lips have been saying 'come and get me' all evening."

"If I may be so bold as to comment, sir, most women like to create an illusion of resistance." He swept away the last of the plates and cutlery and moved on.

Maybe I should try to play the aggressor, be more demonstrative, came Noah's silent addendum. Damn, but I wish it were just the two of us enjoying a candlelit dinner in some quiet little place where we could talk. He watched her fingers rub up and down the tulip-shaped crystal goblet and decided he really didn't want to *talk*. Other things kept preying on his mind. Actually—his lips twisted in a wry grin—they kept preying on his body.

Just as Marlayna decided on the perfect lady for Arthur, he made it even easier for her by announcing that dessert, coffee and liqueurs would be served on the terrace. She nonchalantly maneuvered herself next to another top model, commented on the woman's fabulous complexion and let it casually slip that the Kingman Cosmetics contract was up for grabs. The look of anticipation on the model's face was enough to assure Marlayna that Arthur would indeed be occupied for the rest of the night.

Unfortunately, Marlayna's carefully orchestrated plan for getting Noah off for a private chat fell through. And when she found out that it was a reporter and photographer from *Architectural Digest* who were responsible for the failure of her plan, she promptly erased her mental note to order a subscription. There was nothing for her to do but attend a party that didn't begin to wane until 3:00 A.M.

Exhausted, she took the elevator to her room and tumbled in a graceful heap backward across the wide bed. At first Marlayna thought that she was dreaming with her eyes open. She squinted into the shadows and realized, yes, the fireplace wall was moving. The hearth had swung open. And a surreal white shape was gliding toward her.

6

Marlayna's eyes grew wide and her throat constricted. She had read about haunted castles but had never thought she'd encounter a ghost. Her right hand groped across the pillows to the bedside table, fingers fumbling for the pull on the antique china lamp. When the light bulb exploded the darkness, she expelled a pent-up breath and one word, "Noah!"

"You were perhaps expecting the spirit of Queen Anne?" came his amused inquiry.

She cleared her throat and felt rather foolish. "I was preparing to scream and curtsy." Arranging two pillows behind her, Marlayna watched his slow progress across the huge room, the cane making no sound as the rubber tip was absorbed into the thick carpet.

But it wasn't the cane that held her interest, it was the man. Gone was his evening jacket and tie. The ruffled shirt was unbuttoned to mid-chest, sleeves rolled back to reveal muscular arms. Noah looked invincibly male. The thought made her tingle with delicious anticipation. "Meet anyone else while you were skulking through the secret passages?"

"If you're wondering about Arthur, he's only explored a handful of the hidden hallways. A closet claustrophobic is Mr. Kingman."

"Actually I was wondering about Gwen," she returned tartly. "Maybe you took a wrong turn at the dungeon and——"

"I took all the right turns." Noah settled heavily on the other side of the bed. "Didn't miss any of the signals you've been flashing all evening." He reached down and untied his shoes. "I never knew you were such a tease."

"I haven't the vaguest idea what you're talking about." She primly straightened her dress.

"I'm talking about all those little silent come-ons you do so well with your eyes and lips and hands." After tossing his socks onto the nearby chair, he swung his legs onto the mattress and wiggled into position next to her. "So here I am." Noah's dark brows arched suggestively.

"Like a tomcat who's been on the prowl, finally wandering home and expecting a loving welcome." Marlayna sucked in her cheeks and refused to look at him, staring instead at the slowly closing fireplace. "I don't think you have the right——"

"Right or wrong doesn't interest me at this particular moment." He caressed her from her thigh, along the side of her torso, up her arm to her neck. "*You* are my only interest." His palm curved against her skin, fingers pushing into the ebony curls on her nape. "I can feel the pulse beat of your heart under my hand." He leaned closer, his warm breath fanned her ear. "Beating very rapidly."

"Maybe it's afraid of getting hurt again." Her words echoed the trembling that shook her body.

Noah found himself staring into a pair of very frightened, very vulnerable blue gray eyes. "Never again." His tone was fierce, powerful.

"I need some answers."

"And you'll get them. But not right now." His lips pressed a gentle kiss against hers, lingering long enough to make a silent point. "Now I want you. I need to touch you." His hands moved over her shoulders, pushing down the thin straps of her dress. "Hold you. Kiss you."

His lips nuzzled the curve of her jaw before leisurely moving down her throat. "You smell so good. And feel like silk." His tongue drew a little heart at the base of her throat. "Taste like ambrosia."

He lifted his head, the black pupils of his eyes blocking all the brown. "Suddenly, I'm very selfish. You are all that I desire. All that I need to make me feel complete and happy. I need to know that you love me."

Marlayna became a witness to more than simple masculine sexual hunger. There was no ignoring the anxiety and strain that etched his features, the fear and doubt that clouded his eyes. Maybe a man's emotions could be as complex as a woman's and maybe this time simple action could mean and say more than words.

She slid her hand inside his half-unbuttoned shirt and pressed it against his damp chest. "Your heart is beating even faster than mine."

"Because I'm scared." Noah's hand fastened on hers. "Scared that too much time has passed. Scared that I've lost you. Destroyed what we had."

"I'm afraid, Mr. Drake, I'm a very difficult lady to

104

lose." Her other arm looped around his neck, bringing him tight against her. "Let me tell you a secret." Her low words were whispered into his ear. "Loving you ruined me, spoiled me for any other man. You've shadowed me, lived with me, every day and night for six long years. Long and very, very lonely."

"I suffer from that same disease, but I do know the cure," came his husky rejoinder as his arms cradled her body.

The smile that curved her lips was mirrored in her shining eyes. "So do I." She rained delicate kisses on Noah's face, closing his eyes with kisses, dotting his nose, his lean cheeks and square jaw. Finally her mouth fastened hungrily on his; her teeth nibbled at his sensuous lower lip, her tongue flirting its way inside.

She tugged his shirt from his belt and freely explored the sinewy terrain of his back and shoulders. Touching his tough, firm flesh excited her, sending pleasurable waves coursing through her body. "You feel wonderful." Marlayna half laughed, half cried in delight.

"Let's get rid of this." Noah quickly shrugged off his shirt and threw it on the chair. "And this." In one skillfull move, he swept her dress over her head and tossed it away, only to find it had landed on the lamp, the red material casting a roseate glow around the room.

"What about this?" Her knuckle rapped on his belt buckle, her finger pulling out the waistband of his dress slacks. Marlayna watched his dexterous motions as he easily stripped off the rest of his clothing. "You always could do that with such grace and speed," she said and smiled.

"It's very easy." The palm of his hand glided down her stomach and stopped as his fingers found the lace band on her red panties. "I'll show you." He slowly rolled them down, exposing sable curls, further working them over sleek thighs and slender calves until the silken briefs drifted to the floor.

His memories were replenished by starving eyes that hungrily mapped her nude form. "I didn't think it was possible, but you've grown more beautiful. More desirable." He worshiped her with kisses. His lips moved from her stomach to her breasts and then fused with hers.

His aggressive tongue leisurely toured the honeyed crevice of her mouth and lovingly dueled with its feminine counterpart. His lips rubbed and played on hers, and he moaned with pleasure at once again having access to their sensuous softness.

Noah took a deep breath, trying to temper his frantic emotions. "I love you." Tender fingers stroked her cheekbones and forehead, brushing aside the dark curls. "I always have, Mimi, despite what I did and what you thought. I——"

Her index finger stilled his lips, her voice thick with growing need. "I thought we were going to do all our talking later." Her hand slid from his shoulder to his chest; the dark hair that thickly matted his flesh felt like silk against her palm.

"But maybe we should——"

Cupping her right breast, she lifted it, letting the soft rosy peak tease his hard masculine nipple. "Maybe we should what?"

His hand replaced hers, long fingers caressing her breast, making the stroking circles ever smaller. He watched in fascination as the slumbering nipple crested to full alertness. "Maybe I should do this." His mouth suckled possessively, teeth and tongue tenderly anointing her quivering flesh.

A satisfied moan escaped her as her body became shot through with delicious sensations. "Oh . . . Noah . . . that feels wonderful. . . . It's been so long. . . ." Marlayna pressed his head closer, encouraging him to continue, abandoning herself completely to his lovemaking.

His rough tongue licked at the swollen peak, bathing it gently before his predatory mouth moved on to sample its mate. His hand traveled the sensuous waist-to-hip curve, slid across her stomach and slipped between her thighs. His gentle fingers caressed, stroked and found her moist center.

Her legs trembled, her entire body shuddering under the erotic stimulation. She wanted Noah to share her pleasure, and her hand flowed along his spine, pressing into the hard muscled flesh of his buttocks.

His responding sounds of delight spurred her on, her fingers finally closing over the firm thrust of his manhood. She gently caressed and stroked him, marveling anew at how strong and hard he was yet how like satin he felt against her fingers.

"It has been too long, love," Noah groaned. His breathing was shallow and rapid. "I'm afraid I can't hold out any longer."

"Neither can I." Marlayna pulled him on top of her; her hands framed his face as her legs parted to receive him. "I love you, Noah."

She had finally said the words he had longed to hear. His mouth was harsh, almost brutal against her parted lips. A stunning contrast to the slow, sensual, tender intrusion his body made merging into hers.

Noah savored the moment, experiencing rather

shattering dual sensations of blissful death and brilliant rebirth. "Mimi, love, you've given me back my life." His voice was filled with wonder.

He planted a soft kiss in the hollow of her throat and then his body began to move. "You feel like liquid silk." Long, deep strokes made them both cry out in mutual ecstasy. His hands gripped her hair, his face displaying all the joy and wonder of their union as he continued to bring them closer to their ultimate release.

Marlayna wrapped her legs tightly around his hips and readily matched his desire. Her hands gripped his shoulders, pulling him down onto her breasts, trying to mock logic and science by making two actually become one. Part of her wanted nothing more than to concentrate on Noah, bestowing on him every ounce of love that she possessed; yet another part of her had become selfish and cared only about the pleasure he was giving her.

The tempo of their rhythm increased until Marlayna crossed that elusive boundary and was propelled into exquisite nothingness, a momentary standstill of time that suddenly exploded into a million fluttery pulsations. Seconds later, Noah joined her. His urgent cry shattered the night, he erupted inside her and, with a pleasurable groan, collapsed on her breast.

His arms held her prisoner until his own trembling stopped. Then Noah rolled onto his back, taking Marlayna with him. He pressed her head into his shoulder, his legs sliding intimately between hers, relishing the silken smoothness of her body against his heated flesh. "As God is my witness, I won't ever be able to leave you again."

Lifting her head, Marlayna stared at him. The rosy glow from the dress-shrouded lamp failed to soften the agony that was etched on his features. Hot tears pricked her eyes. She was as confused now as she had been six years ago. "Why did you leave me, Noah? I think it's time for me to know."

Gentle fingertips blotted the moistness from her cheeks. "I don't know where to begin . . ." Noah faltered, "or how. I want to make sure you fully understand everything that happened and why it had to happen just that way."

Marlayna snuggled up, rested her cheek against his and interlaced their fingers. "Start at the beginning. Our fight that awful morning——"

"Had nothing to do with it. I cleverly turned it to my advantage." He rubbed a weary hand over his face. "The accident is the real place to start. There were eight of us working that morning; we were carefully bringing down the east brick wall on the Devon warehouse. And I stress the word *carefully*. Suddenly, the whole damn thing collapsed. Tumbled like a house of cards. Bob, Cliff and Nate just disappeared under a wave of mortar, rubble and dust that ended up swamping the other five of us."

Noah was silent for a moment, thinking about the men he had worked side-by-side with for six years. "I felt like I was drowning. Couldn't get any air, couldn't move, couldn't see. A thunderous roar kept ringing in my ears. So did all the screams." He felt her fingers tighten on his.

"The next thing I remember is an overhead light blinding me. I was in the hospital emergency room. The pain was unbearable. I couldn't seem to breathe. Nurses and doctors were yelling. Needles were being jabbed in my arms. An oxygen mask was slapped on my face. Nothing anyone said made any sense at all. And then, blessedly, everything stopped."

"Stopped?" Marlayna echoed. Her usually smooth forehead was creased by three vertical lines. "Oh, you mean they put you under? Gave you something for the pain?"

He shook his head. "No. Mimi, I died." Noah heard her horrified, strangled gasp. "Hey"—his tone was light, teasing—"it wasn't bad. At that particular moment, I welcomed it. Instant relief. Heaven."

"Oh, Noah, I never knew. They never told me."

"Shhh." His arm slid around her shoulder to give her a comforting hug. "I know, love, I know." He forced himself to continue to sound calm and easy. "Listen, Dr. Pierson was not about to have a mortician steal his fee. He put up one helluva fight over me and Pierson won. Then he busied himself with the real work.

"I had six broken ribs, one punctured lung, internal hemorrhaging from a ruptured spleen and, last but not least, two crushed legs. The legs were the worst, Mimi. The legs were why I had to divorce you."

Noah stilled her lips with his finger. "Please, honey, let me just get through all this." He took a deep breath and continued. "Surgery took care of the lung and spleen. But despite being loaded with antibiotics, the legs developed an infection in the crushed bones. Pierson called in an orthopedic team, but unfortunately all the second and third opinions agreed with the first: If they couldn't clear up the infection and stop the gangrene, both legs would have to be amputated. And even if my legs could be saved, they all agreed, I'd never walk again.

"Being a semiconscious patient was a unique experience," he added with a wry twist to his lips. "They shot me full of drugs to deaden the pain, stuffed me with tubes, wired me into various electronic medical machines and then, they wrongly assumed that I was unconscious.

"But I wasn't. I could hear every word that was said. Groups of doctors and nurses would come in, read the chart and discuss me. Talk about future operations. Banter back and forth about new medical techniques in development. Then the talking dwindled, heads shook, shoulders shrugged, and pity would replace hope.

"Pierson proved to be the most honest of all the doctors. He laid my choices on the line and the line was damn thin. I was the one who had to make the decisions, Mimi. Not only for myself but for you as well. To be honest, the only choice I had was to go it alone."

Marlayna picked her words with care. "How do you figure that, Noah? Didn't we promise to love in sickness and in health?" She came up on one elbow and looked down at him. "I'd like to think that if our positions had been reversed, you would have been there for me."

His hand caught her chin. "That was my biggest problem. I knew you'd be there for me. I knew you'd stand by me at the gates of hell. And I didn't want that for you."

"Maybe you just didn't want me to *wheel* you to those gates." Her anger was simmering. "You weren't just a *body* to me, Noah. Do you think I married you just because of your legs? That I'd leave you because you couldn't walk?"

"No, dammit, and that's exactly why I had to leave you." His finger made a gentle tap on the tip of her nose. "Don't think I was being foolishly macho, either. What I did, I did totally out of love for you."

"Love?" She pulled away and sat up, tucking the

pink quilt under her arms. "I'm not sure we share the same definition of that glorious word. Maybe for you, love is just a physical act. Maybe you equate love and sex. Is love only good, only perfect when the person is perfect? The body is whole?"

Noah stared at Marlayna's bare back, heard the tautness in her voice. He wasn't explaining himself well at all. He cleared his throat and hoped his answers would match his feelings. "Love isn't something you can see. It's an abstract emotion. Sex is much more absolute and visible, especially for a man. I'll admit that during my callow youth, long before I ever met you, the word *love* flowed off my tongue quite easily, with no meaning whatsoever.

"And then, one day, all that changed. You happened. I wasn't interested in a quick score and an even quicker getaway. I wanted to share more with you—all the sensuality and all the tenderness that was buried deep within me not just in the physical act of love but in the day-to-day joys and sorrows, hopes and dreams."

He sat up and put his arms around her, pressing her trembling body tightly against his chest. "I was a man lying to myself about living a full life. I was just going through the motions until you came along. I knew right from the beginning that I would always be more dependent on you than you were on me. You completed me.

"I envied you. In fact I was very jealous of you. You were always the strong one, Mimi. You handled everything and you did it all superbly. When the accident happened, I was forced to make a decision. I was forced to be strong."

Her face rested on his forearm. "And you had to send me away to get your strength?"

"In a way, yes." He laid his cheek against her hair. "My reasoning may seem a little convoluted, but at the time I thought I had the perfect solution. As I told you, Dr. Pierson was very honest about my prognosis, and learning that I was going to be a cripple at best was shattering to both my ego and my manhood. And I will admit, I wallowed in self-pity. Cursed the doctor who gave me back my life. Life?" A cruel laugh twisted the word. "What kind of life was I going to have? I was a prisoner of my body."

Marlayna's hand smoothed the coverlet that shield-ed his legs. "I could have made things easier for you. I know I could have——"

"No. It would have been harder. For both of us. And I couldn't have chanced watching your love turn to pity, then hate." Noah's tongue moistened his dry lips. "There were other factors in my decision, too."

"Like what?"

"Money. We always lived from one paycheck to the next. What didn't go for normal living expenses went for your schooling and my college loan. The operations, medicine, therapy, care and equipment I was going to require went beyond the medical coverage at work. It went beyond any dollar amount I ever dreamed about.

"I knew you too well. I knew that you would work two or three jobs, that you'd work yourself to death to pay the bills. I didn't want that for you. I couldn't watch you die for me. So, I decided on a course of action that would be the best for both of us."

"Divorce." Marlayna couldn't disguise the bitter-ness in her voice.

"Dammit, Mimi, don't you see it was my only choice?"

She twisted around and stared at him. "We could

have discussed it. You could have talked to me, explained yourself." She swallowed hard, and whispered, "You had never done anything to hurt me, Noah. You had never been cruel. And on that day——"

"On that day, I had to be cruel. I took all the anger, all the pity, all the facts and decided to set you free. It may have been foolish, but at that time, in that place, under those circumstances, I felt I had made the right choice. The prospect of losing you was even more disastrous than losing my legs. But watching you wither and die trying to care for me and keep up with the bills, of seeing your love turn to resentment and anger . . . well, that I just couldn't do."

His fingers caressed her damp face, knuckles gently stroking the soft curve of her cheek. "I didn't dare see you again. I couldn't take the chance on losing my courage and letting you talk me out of my decision. The argument that we had played right into my hands.

"I told Dr. Pierson that we were separated, that I had absolutely no interest in seeing you, that you had only come out of guilt, that you were no longer a part of my life. I'm not sure whether he believed me or not, but he went along with it.

"I contacted a lawyer and quickly started all the wheels in motion. I didn't want you to have any association with me, including the same last name. I was afraid that you'd be dunned for money, maybe even have your wages garnisheed."

"Your lawyer was very thorough," Marlayna recounted. "He was also obnoxious, rude, disgusting, demoralizing, crude, horrid."

Noah's lips consumed the rest of her words. "He played his role perfectly." He kissed her again, longer, deeper, more passionately. His hands stroked the tension from her back and shoulders, kneading the soft, supple skin. "I don't know how I ever had the strength to send you away." Pushing the bed linen to one side, he held her tightly, loving the feel of her full breasts snuggled into his hair-roughened torso.

"I wished you hadn't." She playfully tugged a lock of his hair. "I should have stormed into your hospital room and demanded that you tell me to my face that you wanted a divorce. Then we wouldn't have lost six years of our life."

He nipped her shoulder. "Six years. Sometimes it seemed like an eternity, other times like a blink of an eye. But, honey, I'm glad you weren't with me, because I wasn't the same man." At her quizzical expression, Noah gave her a twisted smile. "Time to tell you part two of my story.

"Dr. Pierson and the orthopedic team did what they could for me in Atlanta and then shipped me off to a variety of hospitals including the Mayo Clinic, Columbia Medical Center, Orthopedic Hospital in L.A., various VA hospitals, and every major therapy center in the country. I've got metal and plastic joints and wires in my hips, knees and legs and hundreds of other replacement parts I don't even know the names for.

"I spent most of the years trapped in plaster casts. And"—Noah averted his eyes—"also during that time, I was heavily doped with drugs. Morphine, Demerol, Valium, whatever would make me more comfortable, whatever would make me a more cooperative guinea pig, they shot into me."

Her thumb and forefinger caught his chin, bringing his face back on level with hers. "But you defied them all. You are walking again and free of drugs."

"Very free."

She flashed him a wicked grin. "Apparently those six-million-dollar knees of yours work very well, at least with a mattress beneath them."

"Hmmmm. I guess they did just lose their virginity in a very successful debut. Two years of physical therapy put them through assorted tests but none quite like that. I just began using the cane full time about nine months ago, Mimi. Before that, Perkins would help me navigate my wheelchair around the castle."

"How did you end up here with Arthur Kingman?" came her quick inquiry.

"While I was going through four years of operations and therapy, I finished my architectural studies and passed my exam. I stayed at the VA in Los Angeles for nearly eighteen months and was lucky enough to meet an architect who was volunteering his free time working with patients. He let me apprentice with him and I started doing some freelance assignments. One of them was designing a house for a chemist who worked for Kingman Cosmetics.

"He raved about my work to his visiting boss and Arthur came to see me about the castle. It seemed to be the perfect solution. I could use my skills in remodeling this place, practice with my cane and have a place to live with good old Perkins providing food, minimal care and companionship. And I started looking for you."

Marlayna's eyes widened with interest. "When was that?"

"Six months ago. I tried getting information out of the lawyer you used and failed. Since he was in Chicago, that's where I concentrated on looking for you, but you seemed to have disappeared from the face of the earth.

"I had detectives check out all the hospitals and medical labs, thinking that you were probably doing the same kind of work, but they found nothing. Physically, I was improving and maneuvering better; professionally, working on a project with King Arthur turned out to be a bonanza; but emotionally, I remained a cripple, growing more and more morose when I couldn't find you."

Noah chuckled, his tone self-deprecating. "My black moods, Gwen calls them. I have one drink too many, just sit and stare, agree to anything. That's how I ended up engaged to Arthur's little daughter."

He shook his head, as if to clear it, and then smiled. "When I saw you standing in that hallway, my every dream, every prayer instantly came true. A miracle. A beautiful miracle."

His fingers pushed through her hair; his tough, callous flesh caressed by midnight silken curls. "I'm so thankful that you didn't share my nightmare, Mimi, that you were able to build and enjoy a new life."

"Build and enjoy a new life." Marlayna repeated his words. "Build and enjoy? Build and enjoy!" As her tone grew louder, the phrase sounded hollower. She slid out of his embrace. "Damn you, Noah Drake!" Her balled fist slammed into the mattress, sending shock waves rippling beneath their bodies. "I haven't enjoyed one damn day in six stinking years. And as for building a new life, I didn't do it, someone else did it for me."

His brown eyes widened, then narrowed. "What in hell—I don't—" Noah stammered, then caught his breath. "I think——"

"Maybe you shouldn't," she snapped at him. "Maybe you should shut up and listen." In a defensive gesture, Marlayna protectively clothed her body in the pink eyelet sheet. Her angry expression silently forbade any further interruptions.

When she spoke again, her voice was much calmer. "You know that magazine cover I showed you?" Noah nodded. "Well, that's me." His upturned palms were a sign of confusion. Marlayna made a guttural sound and tried to clarify. "I've been nothing more than a picture of a woman. Flat. One dimensional. More shades of gray than black and white and, unlike that photo, I never had any color.

"I smiled on cue. I pouted on cue. I was a lump of shapeless dough that people molded into the particular form that was needed that day. I enjoyed nothing. Not food. Not clothes. Not people. Each day was a duplicate of the one before—cloudy, overcast, heavy. No matter what the season, that was my atmosphere. And the perfect description of my life."

Marlayna reached for a bed pillow and hugged it close. "The outer me looked perfectly normal while the inner me, the real me, was shattered into pieces. You said I was strong. You said I was secure. Well, I wasn't. I broke. I cracked. I ran away.

"I tried to get in and see you; the security guards threatened to arrest me. None of the doctors or nurses would tell me a damn thing. I wrote frantic, pleading notes that you never answered. Then your lawyer showed up, with his nasty manners and crass insinuations. All our friends suddenly vanished. No one wanted me." She swallowed hard, resolutely trying to halt the formation of tears. "And, silly little me, I kept wanting you."

Noah's chin hit against his chest, his voice a thick, low whisper. "I still feel I made the right decision. Even if you had managed to get in to see me, at that point, nothing could have made me change my plans."

She raised her head, her tone defiant and harsh. "Nothing? How about learning that your wife was pregnant?"

The silence was deafening. Marlayna watched and waited. Noah was staring at her. He made no other movement. Even his chest had stopped rising and falling; he didn't seem to be breathing. She focused on his face and slowly a myriad of emotions were unleashed.

He looked stunned. But astonishment quickly gave way to anguish, a deeper pain than she had witnessed before. And then, Marlayna herself was engulfed by despair. What was the point? A one-upmanship on whose six years had been the worst? Which one of them had been tortured the most? Both of them had sustained heavy losses; ironically both had come out winners in totally different ways.

She extended her arm, holding her hand palm up. Noah hesitated a second and then curved his fingers between hers. "You lost the baby?" She nodded. "Please tell me what happened" came his urgent plea.

"I don't really know," Marlayna said honestly. "At first, I didn't even guess I was pregnant. I thought it was the flu or more likely stress from not being able to see you and then running away to New York. I kept getting sicker and weaker. The woman I was staying with brought me to her doctor and that's when I found out.

"I was so happy and so sure that once you knew, you'd see me and we'd talk everything out. I tried calling you at the hospital, even your doctor, but all my calls were refused. I wrote, but the letters were returned. Your lawyer wouldn't talk to me. I was like a mouse on a treadmill. Running and running, faster and faster but never moving, never making any progress. I decided to fly back to Atlanta, but I never did make it."

She wet her lips and forced herself to continue. "I started to bleed and had a lot of cramping. The doctor put me into the hospital, but . . . there was nothing that could be done."

"I could have done something," Noah grated. "I could have taken your calls." He yanked his hand free, not feeling decent enough to touch her. "I not only lost you, I made you lose our baby." He struggled off the bed. "I killed——"

Marlayna grabbed his arm and held him fast. "Stop it, Noah! You didn't kill anybody." Her fingers turned his face toward her. "There is no blame. It happened. No one was at fault. Just one of those things."

His chest heaved, lungs gasping for air under an enormous emotional weight. "What about you? Are you all right? Any complications?"

"No, I was fine after a while."

Noah looked at her with dawning comprehension. "But mentally, spiritually and emotionally you were——"

"Just as crippled as you were physically."

"We both . . ."

"Yes, we both." There was a finality in Marlayna's tone that sheathed the room in silence, a silence that stretched to nerve-shattering length.

Her fingers were the first to tremble, then her hands, arms, body. That numbing helplessness once again invaded her system and threatened to hold her prisoner. The tears that streaked her cheeks were evident in her voice when she finally spoke. "Noah, I need you. I always have. Without you, I just existed, went through the motions. I didn't live. I didn't want to."

He smoothed her hair from her forehead, gentle fingertips outlined her eyebrows, followed the curve of her cheeks, silhouetted her perfect lips. "I can't believe that you even want me to share your life. Not after what I did, what I put you through." Noah took his hand away. "I don't even feel I have the right to touch you, let alone love you."

Soft palms cupped his face and lowered it on level with her own. "You're the only man who has ever touched me or loved me, Noah Drake. I don't want that to change." She cast him a coy glance. "Besides, why did you think I accepted Arthur's invitation?"

"Well, he is your boss."

"No, I don't have a boss. My contract with Kingman Cosmetics has expired, and I instructed my agent not to renew it."

His dark brows lifted quizzically. "You're interested in remodeled castles?"

"Uh . . . uh." Her fingernail teased a path from his cheek, down the side of his neck to his chest, where it began to draw light circles around his tough masculine nipple.

He cleared his throat and tried not to concentrate on the delicious shivers that coursed his body. "Why, then?"

"When I saw your name linked with Gwen Kingman's, I went crazy." Her eyes flared. "Just the thought of you in bed, loving another woman . . . well . . ." She let her tongue follow the sensual contours of his lips. "I decided to come and cause a major disturbance."

His hands settled in the curve of her waist. "You're doing that right now. Doing it awfully well, too."

Marlayna smiled at him as her hand wandered down his torso, her fingers finding the mole high on his inner thigh. "I haven't even started yet. I just hope those million-dollar knees hold out!"

7

I've heard of breakfast in bed, but breakfast in a sunken bathtub . . . mmmm . . . this is luxury."

Beneath the swirling bubble-coated water, Noah's toes nuzzled the soles of her feet. "After last night my back and knees needed a little whirlpool rejuvenation." A wolfish grin slashed Noah's handsome features. "Let's see what good old Perkins brought us for breakfast."

Pulling the gallery tray along the carpeted floor that flanked the tub, he eagerly lifted the quilted coverings that cozied the food. "Hmmm . . . there are hot croissants in the bun warmer, soft boiled eggs under the egg cozy, fresh strawberries, coffee and assorted jams and orange marmalade." Noah lifted the glass carafe. "Do you still take two sugars and extra cream in your coffee?"

"Yep. Black coffee is one thing Paul has never been able to talk me into."

"Paul?" The sugar spoon stopped in mid-air. "Paul who?"

The odd inflection in Noah's voice made Marlayna stop fiddling with the side water jets. "Paul Wingate. Didn't I tell you about him?"

He handed her a steaming cup. "No, you did not." His dark brows lifted. "As a matter of fact, you haven't told me very much of the day-to-day goings-on in your life. I don't even know where you live."

"I sublet a rather posh duplex on Fifth Avenue in New York. The woman who owns it has temporarily taken up residence in South America until her tax attorney and Uncle Sam can settle a rather hefty money disagreement." Marlayna wrinkled her straight nose at him as she sipped the coffee. "It's not a place anyone could call home. A museum, yes, but not a home. Pearl, the housekeeper, makes sure my fingerprints don't stay on anything for more than twenty-four hours."

"That definitely doesn't sound like you," Noah agreed, adding butter and marmalade to a flaky roll that he had torn in half to share with her. "You were always propping your feet on the coffee table or sitting sideways in that overstuffed tweed rocker we had." A soft smile curved his lips. "I remember the way you would curl up inside that big, fluffy blue bathrobe and sit on the right side of the sofa and read murder mysteries while you listened to the TV, checking occasionally to see if the action matched the sound."

She nibbled on the pastry. "Oh, I still do that." Her eye closed in a conspiratorial wink. "I just make sure everything is neat and tidy for Pearl."

Noah frowned. "Why on earth did you ever move there?"

"Paul found it for me."

124

"Paul again."

Her hands shoveled a hot, foamy wave over his body. "Now don't look and sound like that. Paul Wingate has been my anchor for the past six years. He owns Wingate Modeling Agency but he's more than just my agent, Noah. He's been my friend and benefactor and . . . and . . ." Marlayna hesitated a moment, loath to mention her miscarriage. "He paid all my medical bills and helped me get back on my feet again after . . ." Her voice dwindled off.

Noah stared morosely into his coffee mug. "I'm sorry, honey. I should be thanking the man, not acting like a jealous fool."

"Jealous?" Her eyebrows lifted, her vanity piqued. "What an odd thing to say."

"I'm jealous of all the men you've been in contact with."

"All what men?" she asked curiously.

His right hand chopped the air with vague gestures that sent droplets of water raining every which way. "You . . . you're a model, aren't you?"

"So?"

"What do you mean, so?" Noah knew both his tone and manners were growing more agitated, but he couldn't seem to control his emotions. "I bet there were hundreds of men fawning all over you. Thousands, maybe."

"Millions," Marlayna corrected with a sublime smile. "Didn't I mention that I was in the *Sports Illustrated* bathing suit issue and in their calendar?" She buffed her nails against the blushing swells of her breast. "I was Miss February."

His mouth fell open. "You . . . you're a *pinup?* My wife!"

"Ex-wife," she returned calmly. "And the *pinup*

looks terrific. I had on this nifty bikini. I brought it with me."

Noah snorted. "Don't sound so damn smug. I don't like you being the subject of half-naked pictures, and I don't like the crack about your being my ex-wife either."

She bristled at his superior tone and chauvinistic manner. Marlayna found herself growing more and more irritated and irritable with Noah's take-charge, put-down attitude. She returned her empty cup to the tray and carefully spoke. "I think I have a right to be smug. I'm darn good at my job and in great demand." Her shoulders squared. "I'm going to be thirty this year, and frankly, I've never looked or felt better. If you remember, I was always rather . . . rather frumpy for a twenty-three-year-old."

"Homey. You reminded me of Mom, apple pie and fresh sheets."

Her eyebrows arched; her expression soured. That wasn't the type of compliment she wanted to hear. "I was overweight, didn't know a thing about makeup or hairstyles or clothes. My wardrobe consisted of white uniforms or T-shirts and jeans. I've learned a lot from the various experts that I've met on modeling assignments, and I feel that improving my physical appearance has also improved my self-esteem." Marlayna cleared her throat and added, "And I do happen to be your ex-wife." He mumbled something she didn't catch. "What?"

"I said you look too damn good." Noah enunciated each word clearly. "I'm not the only one who thinks so. You should see the way Arthur drools when he looks at you and talks about you. Gwen said he has plans to make you a permanent acquisition."

"Yes, I know."

He was visibly startled. A vein bulged in the side of his neck. "What the hell do you mean—you know? Has Arthur tried——"

"Of course he has," she returned easily, "but he hasn't succeeded." Marlayna visually caressed the sinewy contours of his shoulders and chest, the bubbles casting a shimmering iridescent glow on his firm flesh. "I'll bet Gwen has tried with you, too."

"I can handle her."

"With tact and diplomacy?" Marlayna inquired sweetly.

"Yeah, with tact and diplomacy," Noah retorted and then his deep voice softened. "I don't think my conscience can justify hurting anyone else."

That rankled her. "Really! Somehow I think both Gwen and Arthur would have to be bludgeoned for anything to short-circuit their own selfish wants and needs."

"You've got a point there." Noah tapped open the top of an egg shell with the bowl of his spoon. "Well, what would you suggest? Keeping in mind that incurring Arthur's well-known wrath wouldn't do either of us any good." He offered her the egg.

Marlayna shook her head and reached for the loofa sponge that was housed in a mammoth seashell that held a variety of decorator soaps, bubble capsules and bath oil beads. She pondered the problem while submerging the beige fibrous scrubber and waiting for it to soften. Slowly her wrinkled brow began to smooth and her frowning expression disappeared. "Maybe I'll just stick with my initial game plan."

Noah squinted at her. "You lost me. What game plan?"

She opened her mouth to explain, then closed it, lowering her eyes from his face to the soap-filled sponge and began to rub at her forearm.

"Mimi . . ." he dragged out the two syllables in her nickname. "Come on, out with it."

Keeping her gaze averted, she reluctantly explained. "I . . . I didn't know what I would find here. With you and Gwen, I mean." She swallowed hard. "I told you before I went kind of crazy when I saw that engagement notice. So . . . I decided if you were physically able to love her, that you could . . . well . . . make love to me too." Blue gray eyes stared into interested brown ones. "Your memory had bedeviled me for six years, Noah, and I thought a little sexual recreation would drive out that devil."

"What if I had been in love with Gwen? What if our engagement was a two-sided one?"

"My plan was to seduce you anyway and plant seeds of doubt in both Gwen's and Arthur's mind about Noah Drake."

His resonant laughter echoed off the tiled bathroom walls. "I'm flattered, Mimi, but you couldn't have done it." His dark head gave a knowing shake. "You just aren't the seductive type. You're too . . . too"—Noah searched for the proper word—"wholesome. That's it. Wholesome and too mature to play adolescent games."

"Seduction is not an adolescent's game, Noah," she said dryly. "A knowledgeable woman can turn seduction into an art."

He wagged a finger at her. "Ahh . . . see, there's the catch, that word knowledgeable." Noah favored her with a sympathetic smile. "Face it, honey, you never were any good at using your feminine wiles. In fact, during the three months we dated before we got married and even after we were married, I was always the aggressor. You were properly shy and sweetly embarrassed."

"Proper and sweet?" Marlayna twisted the loofa between two hands; with each repetition of the phrase, her pride and femininity were dealt a lethal punch.

Noah cleared his throat. "Why do I get the impression you'd rather be wringing my neck than that sponge?"

She threw it up in the air, caught it and smiled at him. "Because it's true."

"Come on, Mimi," he chided, "there's no reason to take offense. You were always a very independent, liberated woman, but sexually you were——"

"Sweet and proper," came her sarcastic addendum. "I don't have to be. I came here without a sweet thought in my head or a proper bone in my body." Her sea-colored eyes were wide and guileless.

His broad shoulders lifted in a careless shrug. "It was an interesting idea, but to tell you the truth, I think I'd burst out laughing any time you went into your so-called seduction act."

"Think so?"

"Forewarned is forearmed." Noah smiled. "Let me think about——" He frowned at her. "Now why are you shaking your head?"

"Because I'm not going to defer. I'm accepting your challenge."

"Mimi, it won't work."

His authoritative tone increased her courage and strengthened her determination. "Oh, yes, it will." Her lashes lowered in a dark sweep. "I bet I could seduce you right now."

Noah moved to cross his arms over his chest,

suddenly stopped to examine his hands and then held them for her inspection. "See these withered, prune-like fingers, that's an exact duplicate of another part of my anatomy. Besides, I'm exhausted from seducing you all night."

Marlayna might have demurred if Noah hadn't capped that blatantly macho comment with a patronizing grin. How like a man to take full credit for a night of pleasure, she reflected silently. How clever of a woman to make him think just that! Dipping the loofa sponge back into the percolating, steamy lather, she marshaled every clever wile she possessed and decided to flex a few feminine muscles. "Oh, Noah, you poor man. Here I've been babbling on and on about utter nonsense when you needed ministering."

Startled by her sudden turnaround, Noah inspected her with suspicion. His wariness, however, rapidly dissolved with just one glance. She looked so soft and vulnerable. Her skin was blushing like a dew-kissed pink rosebud; the humidity had tightened her hair into shiny sable ringlets that sculpted her head. A *cherub*. He gave her a dreamy smile. She was a delightful mix of child and woman with a sweetly innocent face and a gentle, melodic voice.

"Maybe this will help, darling." Shifting her position in the porcelain tub, Marlayna took possession of Noah's left foot, the one with a direct line to his heart, and balanced it on her bent knee. "I read an article that said invigorating the feet through massage can help eliminate body fatigue and actually revitalize a person's entire system."

She used both hands, making sure they were always wet and soapy. Her thumbs massaged firm circles along the callous footpad, moving slowly down the edge of his foot to the thick-skinned heel.

"Mmmmm . . . that does feel wonderful." Closing his eyes, Noah exhaled a grateful sigh and slithered his shoulders further under the water. "My therapist used to do this a lot."

Marlayna began to make subtle changes in her therapeutic technique. The clinical touching became a much more sensual kneading. The tips of her fingers gently rotated over Noah's sensitive arch, her nails whispering across his skin. She continued the feather-light stroking until his toes began to wiggle and his leg tensed.

Noah's brain was late in acknowledging that the hospital therapists had never been able to sensitize his entire body by massaging his foot. He wasn't quite sure what Marlayna was doing, but he was certainly enjoying it. As a matter of fact, he craved even further exploration. Craved! Noah hastily tightened his leg muscles and tried to stiffen and strengthen his resolve.

He vaguely began to wonder whether she was up to something. Noah opened one eye to check but saw nothing more than a woman concentrating all her effort and attention on his left foot. Toes, actually. Her thumb and forefinger were caressing each digit. Caressing and stroking and rubbing and— *No. No,* came his sharp mental directive. *It's just therapy. Impersonal. Hands on feet.*

He silently chided himself. After all, no one in his right mind could get excited over a foot massage. There was nothing erogenous about a foot. Noah swallowed hard as another little current snaked up the back of his leg and ended up giving his solar plexus a pleasant jolt.

She ran the natural sponge across the bones on top of his foot. "I can feel the ridges. Didn't they set well?"

"No." He cleared his throat when that word came

out an octave too high. "The doctors didn't pay a lot of attention to my feet." Noah dropped a few medical terms here and there while he watched her hands slide along his calf.

The more her fingers caressed his well-muscled flesh, the more incoherent Noah became. Marlayna's nails danced playfully against the sensitive back of his knees then began tracing the tendon that tensed in his thigh.

Noah tried to swallow a guttural moan, but his pleasure was too exquisite to control. The childlike play that he had always associated with bubbles suddenly turned very adult in this sultry, steamy oasis. He felt her palms move firmly against his hair-roughened flesh, her fingernails drawing delightful squiggles on that particularly susceptible area high on his inner thigh.

Marlayna decided to diversify and readjusted her position. With the loofa in hand, she swirled the sponge over his flat belly, traveling the path made by the whorls of dark hair that forested his sinewy torso. "You've got the body of a young athlete."

Her hands replaced the sponge, spreading the shimmering lather on his chest and shoulders. Slowly, her wet palms rotated against the tough masculine terrain, the soft pads of her fingers lightly pressed into the whipcord pectoral muscles. "Mmmmm . . . very strong, Noah."

He didn't think it was possible to be destroyed and restored at the same time, but Noah could feel it happening. His entire body trembled. With every word she spoke, her throaty voice conveyed a seductive message. Her hands roamed all over his body, moving from one spot to another, surprising him by going exactly where he wanted them to.

He pulled her closer, his large hands sculpting her body. Fingers and palms slithered wetly as they traced the lush curves of her torso, finally settling in the indentation of her waist. Marlayna floated just above him; her full breasts glided against his flesh, the rosy peaks teasingly hidden beneath a lacy cap of bubbles.

"God, woman, you're driving me crazy." His hands moved to the satiny globes of her derriere and pressed her tightly into him. "I didn't think it was possible." Noah scattered urgent kisses along her jawline to her mouth.

Marlayna turned her face slightly, putting her lips a scant inch away from his. "You didn't think what was possible?" came her purring inquiry.

Noah nuzzled her neck; the delicate scent of jasmine and roses teased his senses. "You know . . ." Groaning words were mumbled as his lips sampled the dewy swells of her breast while the lower part of his body tried to merge in a more vital connection.

"Hmmm . . . yes, I do know," she whispered into his ear at the same time that her feet began to shuffle backward. "But do you *know* that I just seduced you and you didn't laugh once." Her forefinger tapped his nose. "You didn't even chuckle." Delight bubbled in her throat as she watched his lambent brown eyes widen in silent acknowledgment. "I think I'll give the rest of my plan a try."

"Hey!" He made a grab for her but missed. "Wait! You can't go off and leave me like *this!*"

Marlayna eyed him over her shoulder while she wrapped a pink bath towel around her dripping body. "Oh . . . poor Noah . . ." Her tongue clicked against the roof of her mouth. "That's the same line you used in the back seat of your 'seventy-two Mustang when we'd go to the drive-ins." Her lashes lowered in a provocative sweep. "It didn't work then and it won't work now."

She laughed out loud at his muttered curse and scowling expression. "Seduction is the plan for today. Keep on your toes, Mr. Drake. You never know when I'm going to strike." Her fingers fluttered a good-bye wave as she disappeared into the adjoining bedroom.

Noah experienced a few uncomfortable minutes while both his temper and his body simmered. By the time he struggled out of the tub and limped into the Queen Anne suite, Marlayna had already departed. He had no alternative but to make his way back through the maze of passageways that led to his own bedroom one floor down in the west wing.

Perkins was there, impatiently pacing back and forth. "Ah, perfect timing, sir."

"What's *your* problem?" He lifted a dark brow.

"Actually, it's yours." He began helping Noah exchange last night's evening clothes for fresh white slacks and a dark blue knit sports shirt. "Miss Gwen has been frantic. She tried raising you by the house intercom and when that failed came pounding on your door. And when she saw your bed neatly made . . ." Perkins hesitated a moment before adding, "Really, sir, if you're going to keep any more nocturnal rendez-vous, you must learn how to play the game of subterfuge."

A low groan escaped Noah, and he ran a hand over his face. "Why suddenly is everyone such a game master! First Mimi; now you; next me." His eyes clouded. "Perkins, I'm not up to all this; it's not my style."

"Nonsense, sir." He brushed off the collar and shoulders of the shirt. "You're handling yourself brilliantly. Here are your boat shoes. I told Miss Gwen that you had been up and out early and the maid had already tidied your room."

Settling on the massive cannon ball bed, Noah shook out a navy sock and wiggled it over his foot. "What was I up and out early doing?"

"Checking the entablatures on the roof for possible signs of stress along the cornice, frieze and architrave."

"Perkins, I am impressed. You must have been reading some of my books." Noah grinned in approval. "Was Gwen convinced?"

"Thank you, sir, and yes, I believe she was." Perkins stroked the long bulbous line that was his nose. "Mr. Kingman is looking for you, also. Another camera crew has arrived to photograph and video tape the castle." He consulted his pocket watch. "They should be enjoying coffee and scones by the pool grotto at this very moment."

Noah rubbed his hands together. "Okay, Perkins, I'm all set. Let's go."

The house manager paused in opening the wooden door. "May I say, sir, you look extremely fit and healthy this morning."

"Why, thank you, Perkins." Noah lifted his cane, weight-lifter's style, over his head. "Amazing what a good night's sleep can do for a man." His eye closed in a broad wink.

Marlayna decided that the pool was perfect for Aladdin or Ali Baba or anyone else interested in Arabian Nights. A palatial Moorish grotto had been erected complete with handsome brown and white tiles that edged an Olympic-size pool and a shaded cavern filled with waterproof cushioned sofas and chaises.

Ensconced on a bright yellow lounger was Gwen Kingman. A languid "good morning" rolled off Marlayna's tongue as she stretched out on the adjoining chair. "Though I suppose it's actually good afternoon." She smiled and pushed a pair of aviator sunglasses into position on the bridge of her nose.

"Half our guests are still asleep," Gwen returned almost shyly. "Daddy is showing a television crew through the castle and around the grounds. They should be arriving here shortly. The staff is setting up for a coffee break." She nodded toward the group of servants clustered by the far colonnade. "Would you like something?"

"Maybe to share your suntan lotion. I seem to have left mine in my room." Marlayna inspected the blue green plastic bottle. "This is new. I didn't realize Arthur was putting out sun products."

"A trial size just for me," Gwen told her. "I'm very sensitive, and they decided to use me as a guinea pig." She held out her arms for inspection. "I'm acquiring a nice golden glow and not a rash in sight."

Opening the cork top, Marlayna sniffed the contents. "Smells like . . . ummm . . . apricots and coconut." She smiled at the younger woman. "Probably would taste wonderful mixed with gin and poured over ice."

Gwen giggled. "You know, you're very nice and easy to talk to." Her words came out in a sudden rush that turned her face wine red.

"Wasn't I supposed to be?"

"Well . . ." Gwen cleared her throat. "Most of the women here will only give the time of day to a man. And speaking of the male of the species, actually one in particular"—she checked the thin diamond and

136

gold watch that spanned her wrist—"my fiancé seems to be missing. I don't suppose you've seen him?"

Marlayna decided to play dumb. "I don't recall an introduction." When she saw that Gwen was opening her mouth to explain, she hastily interrupted. "Ah, here comes an all-masculine group. Let me guess which one is your intended: the tall blond with the thick mustache and equally thick biceps?"

Gwen giggled again but shook her head, her dark braid swishing back and forth from one bare shoulder to the other.

"Hmmm. No?" Marlayna's brows rose above the sunglasses' frames. "I don't know, Gwen. He's my first choice for you. Are you sure?" Her tone was teasing. "Look at those eye signals he's sending you and that open body language. Why, girl, that man is interested and interesting."

"Do you . . . do you really think so?" came her excited whisper. "That's Randall Porter. He's the youngest man ever to win the Masters Golf Tournament. He did give me a few pointers yesterday on Daddy's course. Randy does have a wonderful grip and swing."

Marlayna smiled as Gwen exhaled a lengthy sigh. "Oh . . . oh . . . I bet it's him. The hunk in the tight tennis shorts. That black beard and macho swagger make him look like a pirate." Marlayna lowered her glasses and winked. "I bet you have some wild fantasies!"

"I do. I do. I mean . . . I mean . . . that's not him either." Gwen coughed and played with the tie on her white bandeau bikini top. "That's Gervaise Saint Pierre, the French perfumer." Her fingers gripped Marlayna's wrist. "He is a hunk and always surrounded by the most gorgeous women. You should see his château in the Loire Valley. That's why Daddy bought this castle; he had to have one that was bigger."

"Not him?" Marlayna pretended to ponder her next selection. "Well, of course, how stupid of me. That's him, the one wearing the snug T-shirt and brief swim trunks. Just look at how bright his big blue eyes got when he looked at you. His face looks very familiar." Her index finger tapped her temple. "I know I've seen him before. Movies?"

"TV," Gwen supplied. "That's Dirk Slade. He's the star of that new spy show that's number one in the ratings. Made the cover of *TV Guide* last week, too. He's signed to do the ads for Daddy's new men's cologne."

"Ahh . . . well, you certainly know how to land a fiancé, my dear. I——"

"Oh, but he's not mine," Gwen returned quickly. "In fact, I bet he doesn't even remember being introduced to little old me. The fan magazines have reported him playing fast and loose with every major female star."

Again Marlayna's ears detected her companion's wistful sigh. "I can't help but notice that your finger lacks an engagement ring. Does that mean it's still unofficial?" Noting Gwen's nod, she continued. "Well, then you're free to take dead aim on any one of those darling bachelors. I'd try the golfer. See . . . he's looking at you again."

"More than likely he's eyeing you," she said softly.

"Me? Hardly. I'm all covered up. You're the one whose gorgeous body is encased in the white bikini." She hid a smile behind her hand as Gwen sucked in her stomach. "That man only has eyes for you."

"Well, it's rather academic. I feel totally tied to the

stake of passion by another man," Gwen intoned dreamily.

Blue gray eyes blinked rapidly behind the gray sun lenses. I was right, came Marlayna's silent rejoinder. Beating her will be the only way to solve this problem! "And who is this charmer that has you so firmly shackled?"

"There he is. Just coming off the elevator with Daddy and the film crew." She turned and displayed a dazzling grin. "Noah Drake, the architect who's redesigned the castle."

"Hmmm . . . I don't know, dear. Your architect looks a bit old and worn out to give you much pleasure. I'd stick with that young, virile golfer. You know, women don't peak until their mid-thirties, while men hit their prime in their twenties. You'll just be shifting into high gear while he's stuck in neutral."

Gwen's cheeks became blotched by ruby color. "I . . . I never thought about that. Noah is fifteen years older than me."

"Fifteen!" Marlayna echoed, her hand clutching her throat. "He could practically be your father. Gwen, you're not looking for another father, are you? A husband shouldn't be his wife's parent. He should be a partner, a confidant, a friend and a lover."

"Yes. I . . . I do want him to be all those things and maybe a little bit more." Gwen gnawed on her lower lip, her smooth brow furrowed in reflection. That was exactly what she wanted, but unfortunately Noah Drake wasn't any of those things—at least not with her.

Marlayna's plans for planting any more seeds of doubt were abruptly terminated when a maid interrupted, talking in urgent hushed tones in Gwen's ear. "Thank you, Patricia, I'll be right there." Her smile was apologetic. "Crisis in the kitchen. Will you excuse me?"

"Of course. We'll get together again later." Marlayna watched her disappear into the elevator. "Tied to the stake of passion!" Her tongue clicked against the roof of her mouth. "I think I may have to drop a bomb on that girl!"

Her gaze wandered over the ever-increasing pool crowd until she located Noah. He, Arthur and two other men had settled inside the covered grotto and were involved in quite an animated discussion. Noting that everyone but Noah had their backs to the pool, she decided to try another feminine exercise.

Marlayna wasn't quite sure why she was acting like this. Perhaps it was being released from six years of pent-up frustrations. Perhaps it was finally being satisfied with herself as a person. Or perhaps it was not wanting to be taken for granted so quickly, wanting to keep Noah slightly off-balance and piqued by her every move.

She was also reveling in a number of private triumphs, especially the way she looked and felt. That in itself provided an all-time high. This was the first time she was enjoying using some of the techniques that she had learned as a model, not only in her grooming but in her handling of crowds of people and refocusing unwanted attention from men like Arthur Kingman.

Once again, her eyes narrowed on Noah. Marlayna felt the need to reestablish herself as a desirable and multidimensional woman. She wanted to tantalize not terrorize, to stimulate him and herself by never becoming complacent and boring. *Mom, apple pie and clean sheets.* She frowned as his so-called complimentary phrase echoed in her mind.

That may have been she at twenty-one but not at thirty. Times had changed and so had she. While having children was very important, there was no reason she couldn't join the millions of other women who combined motherhood with a satisfactory career. "Bought apple pie tastes even better than homemade, and there's no law that says only a woman can clean a house," came her mumbled comment.

Funny, she was just now realizing that a major metamorphosis had indeed transformed Marlayna O'Brian. Her world had once been only black and white, yes and no, right and wrong. Now, she acknowledged that life came in shades of gray with an occasional burst of color, that yes or no was more often *maybe* and that the difference between right and wrong was not as simple as she had once thought.

Her youthful rigidity had softened and relaxed over the years, making her feel freer and deliciously uninhibited—at least with the man she loved. And speaking of the man she loved, one Noah Drake, they did have some heavy communicating still to do, but right now Marlayna was going to use a little body language to send him a message.

Noah didn't notice her when he first arrived and apparently neither did Arthur Kingman, or the man wouldn't have sat with his back toward the pool. Noah saw her just as he relaxed back into the cushioned outdoor banquette. He nodded and made guttural sounds of agreement while his companions conversed, but he kept his eyes on Marlayna.

He held his breath for a long moment, watching her walk along the mosaic tile that rimmed the huge pool. She moved with feline grace, her stride relaxed and her manner self-assured. Noah had expected to see her in a bathing suit but found her wearing a slim white skirt and matching shirt with tails knotted above her belly button.

Little things about her began to fascinate him: the taut, sleek skin bared from her ribs to her hips, the sexy expanse of curvy arms shown to best advantage by rolled sleeves, and the firm thigh glimpsed through the side-buttoned skirt. His gaze was irresistibly drawn to those feminine spots—until she paused by a chaise that was in his direct line of sight and began to unknot and remove her shirt and unbutton her skirt.

Then all hell broke loose inside him. His mouth went dry, his eyes bulged, and his muscles tensed, making his body fidget nervously despite his comfortable surroundings. It took a tap on his knee by the television news reporter to bring Noah back to reality. "I . . . I'm sorry. What was that again?"

"I was wondering if I got these architectural terms correct, Mr. Drake," the sandy-haired reporter repeated. "The castle seems to be an eclectic mix of styles, part Renaissance and part Gothic Revival. And just what are some characteristics of each?" His poised pencil waited expectantly.

Noah cleared his throat and shifted position slightly. By tilting his head, he gave the illusion that he was focusing all his attention on the reporter, when in truth he was concentrating on Marlayna. "Some characteristics of each. . . . Hmmm . . . well . . . you can see the Renaissance traits in the upper stories. Patterns of circles, squares and rectangles are used quite harmoniously."

Pausing while the journalist took copious notes, Noah became mesmerized by the sensual feminine architecture that she was displaying. Her bathing suit consisted of four teeny triangles strung together. Her right breast was sheathed in purple, her left in scarlet, while the bikini bottom was yellow in front and bright blue in the rear. It was a major feat of engineering that rivaled any Noah had ever seen.

"And some Gothic traits?" the reporter politely prodded.

"Gothic? Ah . . . yes . . . hmmmm . . ." His eyes noted the steady rising and falling of her bosom and watched as the velvety swells became slick and glossy under a coat of suntan oil. "Four prime examples of Gothic are pointed arches." Noah swallowed and tried to steady his voice as he continued to follow the progress her hands were making in spreading the lotion.

"Ribs. I mean ribbed vaults." His laugh was as strained as his nerves. Marlayna had greased her stomach and had begun working on the back of her thighs. "And . . . and buttresses," Noah stuttered. "Flying buttresses." He began massaging his forehead with stiff fingers.

"The fourth?" inquired the eager newsman.

"Fourth? Err . . ." Noah plucked the answer from a quick glance at her multicolored bikini, "Ahh . . . stained glass."

"Are you all right?" came Arthur Kingman's quizzical voice.

"Yes . . . uh . . . no." He patted his leg. "Had a rough night. I think the high humidity may be rusting my metal joints."

"Why don't I have our coffee served inside, and we can continue this interview in air-conditioned comfort." Arthur stood up. "I definitely want you to take some film of my library. There's a big screen projection system in there Noah has cleverly concealed behind some carved panels."

Noah deliberately lagged behind as the three men

preceded him through the keyhole archway that led from the grotto into the castle. His increased limp was caused by an ache that had nothing to do with metal knee joints. "So this is the bathing suit that graced *Sports Illustrated?*"

Marlayna fluttered her lashes. "Yes. One nice man wrote that he saved on his heating bill for February by buying extra copies of the calendar."

His fingertip followed the string that spanned her thigh, his voice was husky. "Well, you succeeded in blowing my thermostat, too, and I didn't laugh this time, either." Noah scrutinized the men that congregated around the pool. "I'd prefer it if you'd change into something less . . . less . . ."

"Why? Most of the women here are wearing less . . . less." Her hand rubbed the fragrant oil across her collarbone. "Actually, I'm a bit overdressed. Even Gwen's bikini was less . . . less."

"I don't give a damn about her or any of the others." His tone was sharp. "But you are private stock. Mine. I don't want any poachers."

Marlayna patted his cheek and whispered, "Don't worry, Noah, you're the only one who gets to trespass. You shouldn't keep Arthur waiting; he might come back and see me and . . ."

"Oh, hell. Behave and be good."

"Can't do both." She gave him a push in the direction of the door.

When the dinner gong summoned the guests to the buffet that was set up on the terrace, Noah was relieved to discover that Marlayna was wearing a very conservative outfit. At least it seemed that way until the evening breeze began to press her stunning silk evening pajamas against her beautiful body. Soft mauve splashed with red and silver blue clung in sensuous folds that delineated each feminine curve. It was impossible for him to take his eyes off her.

Noah became more and more aroused as he watched her every move. He wanted to shout to the world that this woman was his, that he and he alone knew all her intimate secrets, that it was only he who had ever shared her bed and knew her love. And he did just that, in the privacy of his mind and heart, while he waited for time to pass so he could end this night in her arms and begin tomorrow the same way.

The clock on the mantel in the Queen Anne suite registered two when Noah pushed the hearth closed. "Mimi, turn on the light." Slowly he limped his way across the darkened room. "Come on, Mimi. You won. Your plan to seduce me all day worked and now it's time to pay up. Mimi?"

His hand groped along the mattress and found the bed linen uninterrupted by a female body. He turned on the lamp and discovered that the bedroom and the adjoining bathroom were quite empty. "Now where the hell can she be?"

8

The passageway was dark and chilly but Noah was becoming extremely hot. His heat was associated with anger, frustration and a modicum of fear. "Where the hell is she?" came his mumbled inquiry as he moved heavily along the upward incline.

During dinner, Marlayna had never been out of his sight. He had enjoyed watching her efficient handling of an ever-persistent Arthur Kingman and had seen her having an extended conversation with Gwen. The topic, Noah surmised, must have been himself, because Gwen had been blessedly distant and preoccupied for the entire evening.

King Arthur's face loomed large in his thoughts. Noah began to wonder if he had somehow waylaid Marlayna after she had said her good-nights thirty minutes ago. "If he dares touch a hair on her head . . ." His fingers clenched fiercely around the curved handle of the cane.

Noah took a moment to rest against the clammy stone walls, trying to steady his erratic breathing while he assessed what he should do next. "I'll enlist Perkins. Maybe he can figure out how to tactfully check on whom Arthur's entertaining in his private suite."

His eyes focused on the amber light that sliced the darkness. The narrow beacon announced that he was approaching the sliding panel that he had wedged open in his room. Using his cane for leverage, Noah pushed the thick mahogany partition to the right and walked into and through the bedroom wardrobe.

"Well, this is something I never expected to see," drawled a familiar female voice, "Noah Drake coming out of a closet!"

Relief made him instantly weak. The anger that followed made him tough and belligerent. "Very funny, Mimi." He ambled to the massive bed where she was sitting Indian-style, filing her nails and wearing nothing but the ruffled evening shirt he had discarded. "I nearly had a coronary when I got to your room and found it empty. Where have you been?"

She flashed him a quick, toothy grin. "Having a little tête-à-tête with Gwen." Marlayna inspected the smooth curve of her nails. "You have that girl tied to the stake of passion." Hearing his disgusted snort, she tossed the emery board on the night table. "Really, Noah, those were Gwen's exact words. As a matter of fact, that seems to be her favorite phrase."

Stretching out on the mattress, she flexed her ankles and wiggled her toes. "So I've been trying my best to tell her that you're not the passionate type, that you're too old for passion."

"Gee, thanks." He hung his cranberry silk bathrobe on the cannon ball bedpost.

"You should thank me." Marlayna came up on her elbow, her gaze traveling the length of his nude body. Her hunger for him was increasing by the minute. "My plan is working perfectly. I've been redirecting Gwen's interest toward that young golf pro, and she has invited him to stay the rest of the week. I've also thought of a way that you and I can be together all the time. Day and night."

Noah settled himself on the bed. "How?" He began to ease open the buttons on her shirt.

"I've decided to hire you as my architect." Her eyebrows wiggled up and down. "Not bad, huh? At breakfast I will bubble forth with the news and off we'll go."

"To where?"

She looped one arm around his neck and pulled him closer. "I told Perkins to put a hold on one of the canopied pontoon powerboats and pack us a big picnic lunch." Her fingers filtered through the truant lock of brown hair that fell across his forehead. "Think of it, the whole day, just the two of us, floating around in the St. Lawrence, talking, laughing"—her knuckles caressed his cheek, the dark stubble feeling wonderfully masculine as it scratched her skin—"and maybe loving a little."

"Speaking of loving, I went to your room to surrender myself into your seductive arms."

She stared into his eyes, the brown irises nearly obliterated by glittering black pupils. Suddenly a deep heat pulsed from her very center, radiating through her body, making her blood circulate faster and her breathing become shallower. "Right now, I'd say you were the one with the seductive arms." Feeling his palm cup her breast and his thumb tease the nipple, she hastily corrected herself, "seductive hands."

"Let's try seductive lips." Noah lowered his head, his insistent tongue thrusting into her mouth as his lips met hers. Her tongue lustily greeted its mate and enjoyed the sweetness of sharing an intimate duel. "All day, you've been just out of reach," he murmured against her mouth, "and it's been driving me crazy."

Her fingertips traced his collarbone. "I just wanted you to look at me and see more than bread and butter." She smoothed the furrows from his brow and wriggled in discomfort. "Oh, it was the damn comment that I reminded you of your mother, apple pie and, God forbid, clean laundry." She gave his shoulder a playful swat. "Stop laughing! Gee, Noah, no woman wants to hear that, especially one who's been deprived of romance for as long as I have. I want to hear words of poetry and passion."

"Didn't you just say I was too old to be passionate?" His teeth nipped her earlobe.

"Actually, what I meant was that Gwen was too young to handle your passion." Her tone was a seductive purr.

"And you can?"

"Hmmmm. I think so." Marlayna's hand moved across the taut contours of his chest. "But what about you?" Her fingers weaved a sinuous trail down his stomach, pausing briefly to circle his navel before trespassing even lower. "What do you think?" She stroked and caressed him, glorying in the virility she had brought to life.

"I think you can handle me just fine," he said huskily. "And I'm sorry that I wasn't more poetic. If you remember, I'm a man of action rather than pretty words."

"What kind of action do you have in mind, Mr. Drake?"

"How about this? . . ." He pressed hot, urgent kisses over her swollen breasts. His tongue circled and stroked a taut peak until it hardened so he could suckle its sweetness. He could feel her slow, sweet trembling.

He journeyed lower, bathing her body with the warm dampness of his mouth. She reveled in the rasping caresses of his tongue against her heated flesh. Her soft whimpers of pleasure invited further exploration.

His hand stroked apart her legs; he kissed the sensitive skin on her inner thigh before the loving lash of his tongue delved deeper into the very center of her femininity. Her body arched as a million tiny explosions turned her blood into molten fire.

She tugged at his hair, pulling his head back up to hers. "Noah . . . please . . . love me . . . now."

In one powerful stroke, his body locked into hers. Their mutual needs were so profound, so intense, that in a matter of a few frantic, wildly ecstatic minutes each conquered and pleasured the other. When his breathing and heart rate returned to a normal level, Noah lifted his head from the curve of Marlayna's shoulder and smiled. "I think I'll take my architectural fee out in trades like this."

"But only with me."

"Most definitely."

"I . . . I beg your pardon." Gwen blinked in surprise, her hand moving to the open collar of her pink knit golf shirt. "What did you say?"

Marlayna smothered her second yawn with polite

fingers, smiled and repeated herself. "I said that after spending two delightful days wandering through the castle, I was so impressed with Mr. Drake's work that we're discussing his designing a house for me."

Gwen looked across the patio breakfast table at her father before turning back to their guest. "I could have sworn Daddy mentioned that you had a place on Fifth Avenue."

"No, I just sublet. I do own a darling piece of real estate in Oyster Bay, and being here"—her arm made a graceful gesture, her voice lilting—"surrounded by the peace and tranquility of water, has made me realize that now's the perfect time to build a place of my own." Marlayna's dark lashes fluttered coquettishly. "Nothing quite as lavish as this of course, Arthur."

His laugh was forced. "I'm sure Noah is very flattered but——"

"Oh, he is," she interjected hastily, "and anxious to learn more about my property and what I'm looking for in the way of architecture. Since no interviews were scheduled today, we thought why not start immediately." Her blue gray eyes looked past Gwen's stricken face. "Here comes Noah now."

She gave her host a dazzling smile. "I know you won't mind, Arthur. We're taking one of the pontoon boats out. You know how important it is to get the feel of the environment." Marlayna's expression turned serious. "This is a major investment for me, and I want to make sure no mistakes are made."

Arthur cleared his throat and dabbed the corners of his mouth with a white linen napkin. "Why do you want to conduct *business* on a boat? Surely, the library would be——"

"Now, Arthur"—she sounded like a teacher scolding a student—"it's important for me to feel the water around me, to embrace its power, to sample its strength. After all, my own property is a peninsula."

"You sound more like an actress trying to live her part than a model wanting a new house," Gwen retorted waspishly.

Marlayna gave her a patronizing smile. "Models are actresses, dear, and I do like to experience life and I will be living that life in my new house. Ahh . . . Noah . . . you're all set. Perkins has already brought our picnic basket down to the dock." She linked her arm into Noah's and ignored the questioning look on his face. "We're off. Bye-bye, everyone."

Gwen's lower lip protruded a good half inch. "I don't like the looks and sounds of this. She was wearing a bathing suit under that white top and tan shorts; I saw the straps. And Noah wasn't even carrying a sketch pad!" Her blue eyes tracked the couple until the elevator door closed. "All this is your fault, Daddy."

"What the devil are you talking about?"

She sniffed. "You were the one who went ahead and put the engagement announcement on the invitations. Since then, Noah hasn't said one decent word to me or even given me a smile and now . . . now . . ." Gwen sniffed again. "Did you see how he smiled at her? I thought you were going to monopolize all Marlayna's time. Instead you've been courting that bleached blonde from California and——"

"Don't you lecture me, little girl," Arthur growled. His fork and knife stabbed and slashed through the last egg benedict on his plate. "What about you? You've been playing more and more golf with Randy, and you were the one who begged me to ask him to stay."

Her hiccups became more pronounced. "Damn . . . nothing is going the way I planned."

"I don't like hearing you swear, Gwen," her father cautioned sharply.

"Damn . . . damn . . . damn." She hiccuped between each word, then lowered her gaze from his narrowed eyes.

Perkins arrived while Arthur was refilling his china cup from the silver coffee carafe. "Excuse me, sir, but here's the list of guests who plan on staying the rest of the week. Ambassador and Mrs. Ferris will be leaving at noon on Thursday. All told, there are twenty-seven in attendance." He handed him a folder. "Cook's menu, sir."

Arthur gave the two neatly typed sheets a cursory glance, nodded and then looked at him, his voice cool. "So, Perkins, I understand you prepared a picnic lunch for Mr. Drake and Miss O'Brian."

"Cook prepared it, sir." He brushed an infinitesimal speck from the narrow lapels on his white suit jacket.

"Don't split hairs, man," came his employer's brusque reply. "See how upset my little girl is."

Perkins's blue gaze shifted to Gwen Kingman. He took note of her red-rimmed eyes and the curled fist pressed against her mouth. "I was following your strict instructions, sir. You did tell me to make sure all the guests' wishes were fulfilled."

He cursed under his breath and scowled. "Sometimes, Perkins, I wonder just who in hell you work for around here."

The house manager gathered up the folder and bowed, his enigmatic expression still intact. "You, of course, sir. I'll tell cook this has your approval." When

Perkins turned and walked away, he was grinning broadly.

"You looked as dazed as King Arthur and Gwen," Marlayna teased as she cast off the boat rope after unwrapping it from around a metal piling hook.

Noah slowly and carefully piloted the boat away from the dock and into the main channel. "Frankly, I was. Still am." He flashed her a broad grin while increasing the boat's speed. "I'm amazed at how easily you handle people, especially those two, with their unique personalities. I've never dared to interrupt Arthur or correct him, even when I could prove him wrong."

Standing in back of the pilot's chair, Marlayna stroked the wide breadth of Noah's shoulders, her fingers loving the contrast of tempered muscle with fine cranberry knit. "I'm a bit more daring than usual because I have you by my side." Marlayna pressed a quick kiss on his jaw.

"I'm flattered, but you were doing all right fielding strangers this past weekend, too. I was watching and remembering how you hated parties. Rooms filled with people, whether you knew them or not, always made you anxious."

Marlayna slid into an adjoining blue-cushioned chair. "Sylvie retrained me. Living with her was like living in a party. She was always ready to have people over or to go out. In her never-ending quest to cheer me up, she would drag me along. I'd end up sitting in a corner, holding a drink I didn't want, while I watched and listened. I guess some of Sylvie's skills rubbed off on me." She pointed to a tiny, tree-clogged mass of green land. "Is that where we're going?"

"Eagle Wing," Noah shouted while he steadily increased the power from the motor. "I'm going to anchor on the southeast side away from the traffic, and you can tell me all about living with Sylvie."

After removing her shirt and shorts, Marlayna settled face down on the blue-carpeted deck in her multicolored bikini. Her hand trolled through the dark green water. "The sun's hot enough, but the St. Lawrence sure is cold." She dribbled water over her back and shoulders. "Hmmm . . . feels wonderful."

Noah stepped out of his white slacks and tossed them over his shirt, which was hanging on the back of the chair. After straightening the waistband of his navy swim trunks, he slowly eased himself down, using the cane for leverage, and stretched out on the deck, so he was face to face with her. "You were going to tell me about this Sylvie person."

"Sylvia Davies. She adopted me on the plane from Atlanta to New York when I ran away," Marlayna explained. A whimsical smile curved her lips. "I think Fate or my Guardian Angel was watching over me that day and put me in the seat next to hers. Otherwise, I really don't know what would have happened to me, Noah."

Her light expression turned ponderous. "You wouldn't have believed what I did. I threw my clothes, which were mostly uniforms, into a suitcase, spent more than I could afford on my plane fare, because first class was the only ticket available, and headed for New York City. I had a bankroll of three hundred eleven dollars and eighty-one cents. I knew no one, had no job prospects and knew less than nothing about Manhattan.

"Sylvia took pity on this air-sick, teary-eyed, bedraggled creature. She fed me a few calming gin and tonics and then listened to my tale of woe." Marlayna shook her head. "I wouldn't have touched me with a ten-foot pole, but she gathered me to her bosom and somewhere over Pittsburgh started to revamp my life. Noah, it worked out perfectly. I was the lost child, and she needed to be someone's mother."

"I owe your friend Sylvie a vote of thanks for watching over you." His fingers twirled through an ebony curl that fell on her forehead. "You could have been eaten alive."

"That's what Sylvie kept telling me as she whisked me off the airplane and into her apartment, where I stayed for three years. Do you know that wonderful woman used to fight with me when I tried to pay something for rent, food and utilities."

"What's she like, Mimi?"

A laugh bubbled forth. "Well, Sylvie isn't the type of woman another woman would want as a friend—at least on first acquaintance. She's the head cosmetics buyer for Lord & Taylor and looks just too immaculate. Perfect makeup, perfect hair, perfect clothes. And Sylvie's the first to admit she's shallow, vain and a snob," Marlayna related.

"But she's so much more. She's warm and loving, scared and confused, and lonely. She's been married three times, has no children and puts all her energy into her career and being a lower-echelon celebrity. Sylvie's kind and compassionate, and there's no stopping her when she gets an idea."

Marlayna's hand went to her hair. "She was responsible for the new me. Kept insisting if I looked better, I'd feel better. So she dragged me to her exercise classes, then down to Lord & Taylor's. Bought me some new clothes, had my hair restyled and sculptured my face with makeup. That's where Paul Wingate first saw me and . . . the rest is history."

"Ahhh . . . so that's how you became the 'Face of the Century.'" Noah stared at her for a long moment. "You know, the short hair, slimmer body, makeup and clothes—well they seem to suit you." He hesitated for a moment. "You've done a lot of changing in six years, Mimi. You're more sure of yourself, more mature and yet you seem . . . younger, more alive. Does that make any sense?"

Her fingers stroked his forearm, combing down the dark hairs that glistened against his sun-bronzed skin. "I was thinking about that the other day. In some areas of my life, time stood still, while I waited and hoped and dreamed about you." Marlayna gave him a tremulous smile. "But you're right, I have revamped not only my appearance but my attitudes and ideas on various subjects. But I've noticed changes in you, too, Noah."

"Physically, of course, but——"

"No, no, other areas, too."

"Such as?"

Marlayna took a deep breath and propped her chin up on top of two curled fists. "You've become . . . ummm . . . less aggressive, almost shy. We've almost totally reversed our positions. You used to love parties and groups and showing off. Now, well, now I get the impression that you could have done without all this hoopla. You shielded yourself from everybody at both cocktail parties." A finely arched brow lifted in speculation. "I was watching you, too, Noah; you didn't talk to more than a handful of people. You were always hidden behind some potted plant or one of those bushes hacked up like a chess piece."

Noah sat up and pulled the wooden picnic hamper

between them. "I'm getting hungry and thirsty. Shall we see what Perkins sent us?"

"You're avoiding my question?"

"I didn't hear one," he returned in a cool tone.

She pushed the top down on the basket and held it closed. "Why are you so reclusive? Surely it can't be because of the accident and needing to use a cane."

"Of course not," came his abrupt retort. He watched her suck in her cheeks in an expression of doubt and strove to calm himself. "Look"—Noah ran a hand through his hair—"when Arthur's around, he likes to be the beginning and end and everything in the middle. Remember, I've been working with the man for two years. I knew better than to try to share the limelight this weekend. He was playing 'King of the Castle,' 'Lord of the Island,' 'Man of the Hour.' I may have been the architect who made it all possible, but on this occasion, I was nothing more than the hired help."

"That doesn't sound like you either." Marlayna frowned. "You'd never let anyone steal your thunder. You'd always——"

"Maybe I've done a little maturing over the years." Noah flipped the top of the hamper back up and held it open with his elbow. "Arthur Kingman happens to be my employer. I have to respect his position."

"Ah . . . but he doesn't have to respect yours?" She reached into the basket and pulled out a wrapped sandwich.

Noah's chest heaved in annoyance. "Mimi, it's not a matter of respecting me. It is a matter of getting recommended for future jobs. Kingman is one powerful man."

"Baloney." When she saw his eyes narrow, she handed him the sandwich and smiled. "I meant lunch, dear. I told Perkins that baloney with mustard and catsup was your all-time favorite."

He ate two sandwiches and drank two bottles of Canadian lager without saying another word. Marlayna thought of trying to tease him out of his mood but then decided to wait Noah out. She attacked her shrimp-filled croissant with hungry zeal and cautiously sipped at the ale. The slightly bitter beverage proved to be the perfect drink to quench her thirst during the heat of the day.

"You know, Mimi, the castle was my very first independent architectural project." Noah absently massaged his thigh. "Most of my fee went to paying for my therapy bills. The rest I put into high-interest certificates so I could be increasing my money while I lived on the island."

For the first time, he ventured to look at her. He spoke his words with care and hoped that she would understand his concerns. "I want to open my own office and all the publicity that Arthur is generating will, I hope, make people trample their way to my door." He ran a hand around his neck to mop the perspiration. "There are some people who demand respect but don't ever give any in return. That sums up Arthur Kingman. He can be vicious when crossed. I have no doubts that he could easily decide that all my design work is substandard and publicize the same. That would ruin me."

"Even though it's false? Surely——"

"People always remember the first and the worst," Noah pointed out, "never the retraction or the vindication."

Marlayna handed him the rest of her ale to finish. "I suppose you might have a point in the case of King Arthur; everyone always walks on the proverbial eggshells when he's around." She shivered despite the intensity of the late afternoon sun. "I'm glad I decided not to renew my contract with him."

"I'm glad of that, too." Noah leaned over and kissed the tip of her sun-pinked nose. "I don't want Arthur Kingman anywhere near you."

"I don't think we have to worry." She smiled and stroked his cheek. "I cleverly let it slip to Claudia Wells that the contract was up for grabs, and she's been acting like Arthur's Siamese twin these past few days."

"Oh, so that's who that willowy blonde is." His eyes widened appreciatively.

She pretended to be annoyed. "And what are you doing noticing willowy blondes, Mr. Drake?" Her fingers moved from his shoulder to tug at the waistband of his bathing suit. "Maybe you need something to keep your mind occupied."

"You just might be right." Noah pulled the strings that held the top and bottom of her bikini in position. The four colorful triangles drifted onto the deck as he gathered her into his arms and proceeded to keep both their minds and bodies occupied.

"Ohhh . . . that feels wonderful. What is it?"

"Perkins's homemade sunburn remedy. Smells like a sandwich spread." Noah held the Mason jar under her nose so she could sniff the contents.

"Then it's the perfect thing to spread on my burned buns." Marlayna flashed him an impertinent grin. "I didn't think I was going to make it sitting through dinner. Doesn't Arthur ever serve hot dogs and hamburgers so people can stand around the barbecue?"

His hands slipped and slid as they coated her velvety buttocks with the thick lotion.

"Stop laughing," she grumbled. "This was all your

fault. You said your bionic knees couldn't take the hard surface of the boat deck. So I made the supreme sacrifice of baring my delicate parts to the sun—and do I get any thanks?"

"As I recall, you screeched your thanks so loudly that you disturbed a flock of snow geese."

Marlayna turned her head and stuck out her tongue. She cradled her head on her folded arms, sighing gratefully as he continued applying the cream. "I never appreciated a crowd so much as I did tonight. Talk about a cold shoulder—Arthur and Gwen were barely civil to me. You, I noticed, were not on the receiving end of the icy stares and curt conversations."

"That's because you were being so naughty! I'm positive Gwen saw you kissing me when the elevator door opened."

"I kissed you at every floor hoping that someone would see me." She rolled on her right side and smiled at him. "That's why I decided to not so subtly sneak into your room tonight. That Italian dress designer wagged his finger at me and winked."

Noah towel dried his greasy hands. "I could have used the passageway to your room. Wouldn't it be more tact——"

"Don't you dare say that word!" Marlayna warned. "Tact and diplomacy will only keep us apart another six years. Besides, I think Gwen is leaning on that golfer a little bit more each day, and Arthur can't seem to stand up without Claudia propped under his arm." A Cheshire cat grin formed. "I'd say my plan is working wonderfully."

9

I don't like these people, Noah." Marlayna's hands curled over the edge of the wooden dock, her feet kicking into the dark green water that roughly assaulted the moorings. "Only two more days until this week ends. I can't wait."

"You've said that at least twenty times since we left the castle." He swatted his neck, rejoicing in the death of yet another pesky mosquito, and wiped his hand on his khaki shorts.

Noah looked from the blue pontoon boat that was jouncing in the rising river over his shoulder at the gloomy, heavily forested landscape. "I don't know why you wanted to picnic at this end of the island. It's like a damn jungle, steamy and insect ridden. We should have stayed put today."

"So you keep saying." Her voice reflected a change in her mood. "What's the matter with you, anyway?

You've been acting . . . I don't know"—her shoulders twitched—"itchy for the past few days."

Noah stared at her for a long moment. "Nothing. Everything." He took a deep breath. "Maybe it's the damn weather." He looked at the black-bellied clouds that were battling for control of the azure sky. The elements were bent on confrontation, and that seemed to echo everyone's mood. "A storm's been threatening since Wednesday."

Marlayna rolled her eyes. "And not only from Mother Nature! Arthur and Gwen have been raging at me by word or deed since Monday night."

"Your outrageous hijinks are probably getting on their nerves." He downed the last mouthful of cold beer and put the empty bottle in the picnic hamper and extracted another full one.

"Nothing's been that outrageous," she protested and then gave him a sly smile. "You haven't complained. So they caught us in the swimming pool at midnight without our bathing suits. Or was it we who caught Arthur and Claudia trying to do the same thing!

"And what's a little dancing in the hallways at three A.M.? My negligee was perfectly respectable." Marlayna wagged her finger at him. "Besides, what was Gwen doing up at that hour with the golf pro? I'll bet he wanted to play more than golf."

"Don't be crude," Noah cautioned. "Gwen's a nice kid."

"I didn't say she wasn't!" Marlayna struggled to keep the defensive tone out of her voice. "She and Randy seem to be progressing into a wonderful relationship. Didn't you notice how protective he was of her?"

"Some women inspire that in a man."

Marlayna opened her mouth, then closed it, deciding to let his obscure comment go unchallenged. "What's Arthur been saying to you?"

"Not much. He's pretty annoyed and was very curt with me during the *People* magazine interview yesterday. He asked if I had any rough sketches for your house. I told him that you still hadn't been able to make up your mind, that you were still getting the feel of the environment."

She popped a green seedless grape in her mouth, enjoying the instant squirt of refreshment that the slightly tart juice provided. "Oh, but I do have an idea, if you want to sketch." At his silent query she explained. "I did this photo layout in California and fell in love with a stilted beach house I saw in Malibu. It was really lovely, Noah. There was a panoramic view of the ocean through a wall of windows. It had four bedrooms, den, kitchen-family room, living and dining room. I'll defer to your judgment, of course, but I think it would be the perfect choice for my beach property."

He choked and sputtered as the beer hit the back of his throat the wrong way. "You . . . you"—he coughed and cleared his throat—"you mean you really do own property on Oyster Bay?"

She nodded. "I also have a condo in the Bahamas, which I rent, and land in Hawaii." A grape was halted about an inch from her mouth. "That's on the ocean, too. Mmmm . . . oh, and Paul just closed a deal on land in Arizona." Marlayna gave him a happy smile. "You could just keep busy designing homes for us!"

In an oddly high voice, he asked, "Do you own any other real estate?"

"I have other property, but nothing that you could

build on. You know," she blithely rattled on, "tax shelters—offshore oil leases, gas drillings, low income housing partnerships and . . . ummm . . . equipment leasing investments. Every so often my business manager——"

"Business manager!" Noah echoed.

"Uh huh . . . well, he likes to experiment. This year he decided to try a cable TV franchise. It proved to be an excellent investment."

He mumbled something that she didn't quite catch, and when she inquired he just waved a hand at her. His thoughts were a chaotic jumble, a myriad of questions. Noah held his breath and asked the one that was most overwhelming. "Mimi, exactly how much are you worth?"

Her feet fluttered in the water. There was an underlying tension in his voice that puzzled her. She decided to be vague. "It . . . it changes."

"I don't think the IRS would appreciate that type of answer on your tax return," came his sarcastic rejoinder. "How much was your Kingman contract?"

"Nearly a quarter of a million."

"And you did other things?"

Marlayna nodded. "But not everyone paid that much. Paul charges about fifteen hundred an hour for me, although I did get ten thousand for a pantyhose print ad." She lifted her feet out of the water and wiggled ten primrose-lacquered toes. "Two weeks ago, I did some fur coat ads and before that . . ."

Her voice droned on and on, but he had stopped listening. His eyes became riveted on legs that were displayed to best advantage by brief white shorts. He examined every facet of their appearance. Her feet were narrow and smooth, not a callus or blister or ridge in sight; her ankles were trim and graceful; legs long from ankle to knee and from knee to hip. Long. Slender. Curved. Sleek. Silky smooth skin tanned to a satiny bisque.

Noah scrutinized his own legs. They looked short and stubby next to hers. His four extra inches in height came from his torso rather than his legs. *His legs.* What god-awful sights they were. Red scars snaked his shin and calves, checkerboarded his knees and slalomed his thigh. Angry scars that never seemed to fade or even to be concealed by the dark curls.

"It appears that we both possess million-dollar bodies," he interjected in a strained voice. "I bought mine, while other people pay you for yours."

Marlayna gave a philosophical shrug. "This year they pay. Who knows about next year? Modeling is much like fashion. What's *in* now is *out* in a blink of the camera's eye. My name is at the top of everyone's list, but it can quickly be replaced and forgotten. Paul has been negotiating a lucrative 'switch' contract with one of Arthur's competitors." She patted her cheek. "So it looks like the 'Face of the Century' will be around for another season."

"You're going to continue with your work?"

Again she was aware of the rawness in his tone and deliberately made her own voice soft and gentle. "Well, Noah, I do have quite a few bookings on my schedule and there are a few contracts pending."

He wiped the condensation off the short neck and body of the green glass beer bottle. "But after that you're free."

"Technically. I do have this new cosmetic campaign——"

"But that contract hasn't been signed."

166

"Not yet."

Brown eyes locked into her blue gray ones. "I'm hearing more yes than no." She nodded. "How strange. Somehow I got the impression that modeling didn't mean anything to you. That you laughed and smiled and posed on cue."

"Maybe I just didn't explain myself too clearly."

"Then please enlighten me."

She ran her fingers through her hair, lifting the damp sable curls that molded her nape. "I . . . I guess I just didn't realize how it had turned from a job into a career." She hesitated a moment before adding, "Modeling is not my life, Noah, but I do have obligations, very lucrative obligations that will give us financial freedom for the future. Right now I'm at the top and I do feel I should take advantage of it."

"You're on top and I'm on the bottom."

She frowned. "That's an odd thing to say."

Noah flicked another flying insect from the sleeve of his brown polo shirt. "Odd but true."

Marlayna's own anxieties began to increase. She decided to joke Noah out of his mood. "My position on top is a very precarious one, while you've cemented yourself a very impressive foundation. The kudos that are coming your way from your work on the castle will send you to the top, too. Offers will be pouring in from around the country, around the world." She squeezed his knee. "I bet you won't be in your New York office more than two days a week."

"New York office?" One dark brow lifted quizzically. "I'm based in Atlanta."

"Well, two days in one office, two days in another." Her smile was bright, her tone breezy. "Thank goodness for jets. At least you'll be home every night."

"And I assume *home* will be in *your* duplex or on *your* property in Long Island."

"Since when did *we* ever mark things *yours* and *mine?* We always threw our work efforts into a shared pot marked *ours.*"

A muscle twitched in his jaw. "I don't have anything to contribute to *us.*" Noah stared at his legs. "I don't have much to contribute to myself, let alone someone else."

His eyes returned to her; he watched her smile fade. "Let's face it, Mimi. You've got it all. Everything. What you don't have you can buy. What use am I to you?"

She pulled her feet up, rested her cheek on her knees and tried to stay calm and logical. "All right, Noah, let's get everything out in the open. Tell me what's bothering you." Marlayna viewed his chiseled profile, taking note of the pinched nostrils and thin line of his lips. "Why are you talking such nonsense and acting so different?"

"Different?" A hollow laugh reverberated deep in his chest. "I'm not the one who's different."

"And I am?"

"You said it, lady. Everything about you, from your hair to your painted toes and in between, is different." His hand made wild, vague gestures that sliced the air. "Your manners, your attitude, your actions, even the way you talk. I've grown more and more aware of it every day." Noah's dark head nodded. "You've changed, Mimi. You're complex and complicated. You keep denying it, but it's the truth."

Her hands clenched, the knuckles showing white. "The only thing that's changed, Noah, is the way you see me. Or maybe it's the way you see yourself."

"What the hell does that mean?" His words were forcefully expelled.

She fought for strength and control. "Your little comment about being on the bottom."

"I am. I've had to start all over again, not only with a career but learning how to live." His teeth clamped down on his lower lip, his eyes empty as they stared but didn't really see her. "I'm realizing just how far you've gone without me. You're strong, competent, capable and talented. I was a fool to think we could pick up where we left off. The only thing that has remained the same is our sex life."

"And you think that's all I want you for?" Her voice increased in volume. "Sex?"

"What else can I give you?"

"Dammit, Noah, I didn't have to wait six years for sex!" she shot back ruthlessly. "I don't understand this sudden slide of yours into despair." Marlayna counted to ten and strove to be calm. "Noah, we're finally together; we've got everything to look forward——"

"Forward?" His head snapped up. "Not with me, Mimi. With me you'd be going backward. I'd only cripple your life."

"Ahhh . . . so that's it! Noah Drake the noble *cripple!*" Marlayna pounced on his word. "Is that the way you see yourself. As a gimp? A failure? Half a man?" She kept hammering away, hoping that Noah's own anger would erupt and this confrontation would cleanse away all doubts.

He felt a rush of blood to his face; nausea curled his stomach. "It's the truth."

She looked at him and slowly shook her head. "I don't believe you," Marlayna shouted. "You were the one who said he couldn't stand to see pity. Yet pity seems to be exactly what you want from me."

Her hand caught his chin. "Well, I'm not going to give it to you. Why should I? You seem to be manufacturing an abundance of it for yourself. Wallowing and moaning, poor Noah Drake."

Roughly, she pushed his face away. "And I'm not going to be strong for you either. You've got enough strength buried inside of you for ten men or you couldn't have come this far." Marlayna took a deep breath. "No . . . somehow, someplace, somewhere you've lost your strength and your courage. Noah, only you can find it."

"I . . ." His hand rubbed the perspiration from the back of his neck. "I . . . need time. Time to think about us." He lifted bleak eyes.

"Do you? Fine." She brushed off her hands, stood up and towered over his hunch-shouldered form. "You take all the time you want. When you make up your mind, you let me know. And if you're lucky, I won't have changed mine!" With that, Marlayna sprinted down the dock to the boat.

"Hey!" Noah scrambled to secure his cane as he saw her untie the mooring rope and jump inside behind the wheel. "Mimi! What the hell!" He heard the engine turn over. "Wait! What are you doing? Mimi!" In his struggle to stand, he lost his footing, knocked the picnic basket into the water and fell heavily onto the dock. "Mimi! Help me."

Marlayna closed her eyes to the scene. It took all her willpower not to run to Noah's side. But what she had told him was the truth; she couldn't be his strength or his legs. He had both. Now all he needed was the chance to realize that fact. She shifted the boat into high gear, jouncing along the rough caps as she followed the coastline back to the castle.

Sprawled on his back and struggling to control his violent breathing, Noah waited for her to return. He concentrated his attention on sound, listening for the pontoon boat's engine to slow down and reverse itself. But that didn't happen.

"She just needs to work out her anger," he told himself calmly. "I remember that one fight we had. Mimi was so mad that she climbed in the car and laid rubber all over the driveway. Ten minutes later, she was back, clutching a speeding ticket, crying and feeling foolish."

Ten minutes came and went. So did another fifteen. Noah was the only one feeling foolish. He finally managed to pull himself to his feet when the rain started. At first the warm droplets just dimpled the water. A few seconds later, he was assaulted by large stinging droplets that soaked him.

Gwen Kingman interrupted the hushed conversation between two of the upstairs maids. "Libby, when you've finished picking up the guests' laundry, you'd better start turning on some lights." Her gaze swept the hallway. "These corridors have all the ambiance of a tomb."

"Yes, miss." The young woman shifted uncomfortably.

"Is there something wrong, Libby?"

"Well, I . . ." Libby looked to the other maid for guidance, received a vigorous nod and stammered anew. "I . . . I really don't know what to do, miss. I don't want to lose my job." Her voice lowered to a whisper. "I don't want to cause no trouble, either."

"Maybe I can help." Gwen patted her hand. "Is there a problem with a guest?"

"Just his laundry, miss."

"Whose laundry?"

Libby cleared her throat. "Mr. Drake's." She pulled two items from the canvas duffle bag. "Should I return these to his room or ask him who they belong to?"

Gwen stared long and hard at the two items. Two very feminine items. One was a pair of black silk bikini panties edged with red lace; the other was the bottom of a bathing suit—yellow and blue triangles—that she had seen before. "I know who they belong to, Libby." She snatched the clothing off the cart. "I'll see that they are returned to their rightful owner." Her posture regal, she strode swiftly down the corridor to the elevator that would take her to her father's study.

"Daddy!" Gwen flung open the oak door, startling Perkins, who was on the library ladder, into dropping three books. "This is the final insult!"

Arthur spoke quickly into the telephone and hung up the receiver. "What the hell is your problem, little girl? Where are your manners?"

"Why should I be the only one with manners?" She threw the clothing on his desk. "It's obvious your Miss O'Brian has no manners or morals either."

He picked up the panties. "Because of her lingerie?"

She gave an unladylike snort. "Her lingerie was found in Noah's room!" Gwen's foot beat a furious tattoo against the Oriental carpet. "I'm no fool, Daddy. I know what's been going on. I won't close my eyes to their tawdry affair any longer. I want that woman out of this house and off this island. And I want it done now!"

"What about Noah? It takes two to have an affair," Arthur pointed out.

Gwen cleared her throat. "I'm trying to be very adult about this, Daddy. Noah may just be temporarily blinded by the woman." She turned her head when an oddly strangled sound was emitted by Perkins. Her eyes scolded him. "Daddy, I think if we remove temptation from this house, perhaps Noah will be more his old self."

Arthur massaged his jaw. "He has been acting out of sorts lately. Not at all like himself. Perkins, where is Miss O'Brian?"

"She and Mr. Drake are out on the boat, sir."

"I want to know the minute her foot hits the drawbridge, do you understand?"

"Very good, sir." Perkins dutifully left the room.

About four miles up the coast, Marlayna crossed an invisible boundary line. The bow of the boat was wreathed in sunlight while the stern of the boat was still being splashed by rain. She increased speed as the sky rumbled continuous warnings.

Green channel markers guided her on the port side and once the rose granite castle loomed in sight, Marlayna slowed the engine and trolled close to the shore until she saw the summer house on the main dock. She cut the engine a bit too late and the bow of the boat slammed into the dock. "Oops. Sorry about that."

Marlayna mumbled to herself all the way up the stone steps. Maybe she should go back and get Noah. After all, he was eight miles from the castle and it was raining and his legs— She stopped. His legs were fine, his brain was the only thing that was crippled. Maybe a long walk in the pouring rain would wash out those macho cobwebs that had been collecting for six years.

The instant the front door opened, Perkins stopped pacing. "Ah, miss, I . . . I have some bad news."

"That makes two of us." She folded her arms

across her chest. "The picnic basket deep-sixed into the river, I smashed the boat against the dock and Noah"—Marlayna exhaled sharply—"Noah is walking home."

"Walking? Really, miss, don't you think——"

"At this point, Perkins, I've stopped thinking and started acting. He's perfectly healthy and his knees won't rust." She laid a hand on his arm. "He needs to think about his future and mine." Marlayna coaxed her lips into a smile. "Now, what's your bad news?"

"Arthur and Miss Gwen are waiting for you in the library. It seems your lingerie was found in a most compromising location."

"Is that a fact?" She straightened her black sleeveless cotton shirt and brushed down her white shorts. "Well, Perkins, let's go beard the king in his den."

The house manager groaned and rolled his eyes. "Miss O'Brian has returned, sir," he announced rather unnecessarily as they entered the mahogany-paneled library.

"Stay a moment, Perkins," came Arthur's presumptuous order. "Miss O'Brian will be needing your assistance in packing." He looked at the gold watch on his wrist. "Captain Warren will be arriving in ten minutes to take you back to the marina. A cab will take you to the airport."

Marlayna smiled first at Gwen then at her father. "Arthur, I see you don't go in for long, melodramatic good-byes."

His brow raised in acknowledgment of her flip tone. "I see, however, that you do go in for nocturnal recreation." Arthur held up the black panties between his thumbs and forefingers and stretched out the waistband. "I overlooked that night at the pool, but this——"

"Night at the pool!" Gwen echoed. "What night at the pool?" she demanded. When her father didn't answer, she began to snivel. "Dad—dy, you knew? You . . . you knew th—they were carrying on?"

"Don't cry, Gwen." Marlayna's voice was low and comforting. "Noah and I were carrying on long before either of us ever knew the name Kingman existed."

Arthur pushed himself out of his red leather executive chair. His shoulders were pushed back, posture rigid as that of a four-star general being reviewed by the president. "Well, the name *Kingman* does exist, my dear. And it's a name that demands respect. It's a name of power and position."

His palms were pressed flat against the glass top of his massive carved desk. "A name that you will no longer have any dealings with. You do understand."

She nodded. "Perkins"—Marlayna turned her back on the Kingmans—"shall we get to the packing?" Without a backward glance, she left the room.

"What about Mr. Drake, miss?" Perkins repeated for the fifth time while Marlayna bustled back and forth from the bathroom to the closet to the suitcases that were lying open on the bed. "I really should go and find him."

"Just leave him alone. He has to win this battle for himself. Maybe a trek across the island will prove to him just how strong and capable he really is."

"And when he finds you're gone?"

"Noah will have to deal with that, too. He knows where he can find me if he wants to." She jammed her shoes into the side pockets and flipped the lids over to zip them closed. "But he's got to do the wanting and the finding."

Marlayna's fingers pressed against his cheek. "Perkins, you've been wonderful." Suddenly her arms wrapped around the startled manager's neck. "I'm going to miss you." She sniffed and wiped her eyes. "You take care of yourself and . . . Noah."

"I always have, miss." He patted her shoulder. "You take care, too."

At three o'clock Captain Warren deposited her at Blind Bay Marina. The twenty-minute crossing was calmer than she had expected. There was no wind and the constant drizzle seemed to have flattened out the river. Marlayna's thoughts were preoccupied not with the weather or with her chattering seatmate on the shuttle plane from Ogdensburg to Albany, but with Noah. She was wondering if all that had happened would put an end to their future together.

Noah ran out of swear words after the first hour. His clothes were dripping, hair plastered to his head. He was hot and covered with bugs, and everything that could hurt—hurt. His cane was more a hindrance than a help—the rubber tip kept sinking into the mud—so he used the trees for support.

The sun shone through the gray cover of clouds. It kept sinking further and further westward. He had no idea how far he had walked, but he knew that he had a much longer road to travel. A road that had nothing to do with dirt and pine needles.

10

Three days and nothing! Not even a phone call."

Sylvia Davies rolled her eyes and sighed as she watched Marlayna lift the receiver for the millionth time to check the dial tone. "No wonder he can't get through, you keep interrupting the connection." She went back to filing her nails. "Relax, the man probably hasn't finished drying out yet. For heaven's sake, stop pacing! You're wearing a hole in the carpet, and you know how traumatic that would be for Pearl."

Marlayna flopped on the sofa and buried her face in her hands. "I made a terrible mistake, Sylvie. I shouldn't have run out on Noah. I shouldn't have left him at the other end of the island. I shouldn't have let Arthur bundle me off. I should have——"

"My dear, life is filled with shoulds and shouldn'ts," Sylvia interrupted. She put her hand on the back of Marlayna's head and stroked the disarrayed curls into calm order. "The one thing you really shouldn't do is to keep going over it."

A wry smile peeked through fingers. "No crying over spilt milk? I made my bed and now I get to sleep in it. All alone."

"I don't think you could have found a bed big enough to accommodate you, Noah and his self-pity."

"I wish . . . I just wish"—she wiped her hands over her face—"that I had had enough sense to keep my mouth shut. Talk about stupid! But oh, no . . . I thought I was so damn smart. Noah needed reassurance. He needed love and support, and maybe he did need the pity. I should have told him what he wanted to hear, and then, once we were together and he was more confident, I could have gotten some professional counseling on how to handle his emotional needs."

Marlayna turned her head. "The man went through hell for six long years, Sylvie. And did I appreciate his situation? No! I was too concerned with . . . frivolities like his engagement and the Kingmans and . . . and"—she hesitated a moment—"and getting some gratification for myself. Oh, damn, I really bungled everything." She wrapped her arms around herself and began to rock to and fro on the sofa cushion.

"Oh, honey, now don't do that." Sylvie pulled her against her breast. "I bet it's just a matter of time before that bell rings, you open the door and there he'll be!"

Suddenly the bell did explode the silence, and both women jumped to their feet and raced for the door. Marlayna's fingers trembled as they pushed down on the French latch. "Oh, it's just you, Paulie." She collapsed against the door frame.

Paul Wingate managed a feeble smile. "What a warm greeting for the man who's taking you out to dinner." He lifted Marlayna's chin and assessed the damages. "Hi, kiddo. I hate to say this, but on you even dark circles look good." He glanced at Sylvia. "Isn't she sleeping at all?"

Sylvia shook her head as the trio went into the living room. "She does have rocking and pacing down to a fine art. But going out to dinner should perk her up. Why don't we try that new Hungarian restaurant that opened to great reviews in the Village?"

"Sure, why not." Paul rubbed his hands together. "My ulcer's been kicking up all day on bland food; might as well give it something to really burn about." His blue eyes focused on Marlayna's dejected figure. "Come on, Sylvie, let's get her out of those worn jeans and that T-shirt and throw some cold water on her face."

"I'll rearrange her hair and daub on a bit of makeup here and there and she should be just about presentable."

Marlayna looked from one to the other. "It's really amazing the way you both talk about me as though I'm not here."

"You're not," Sylvia returned. "Your body might be, but your mind and heart are off—" Her hand fluttered gracefully.

"I know." She twisted the bottom of her navy cotton shirt between her fingers. "Listen. Can't we just eat here? I just don't have the energy to tackle the Village or other people. Pearl stuffed the fridge and cupboards with all sorts of goodies." Hearing their muttered "okays," Marlayna grabbed Sylvie's hand. "Come on, maybe we can toss everything into a single pan and come up with goulash."

Paul groaned and reached into his pocket for another antacid. "Oh, hell, this is the last one. Marlayna, do you have any?" He held up the empty wrapper. "This damn ulcer——"

"Erupted when Arthur Kingman called on Saturday," she finished for him. "I'm sorry, Paul." Marlayna squeezed his arm. "You shouldn't have had to take the brunt of Arthur's wrath."

He gave a reminiscent grin. "It was worth it. I always wanted to tell that pompous, overbearing, stuffed piece of pseudo-royalty where to go." Paul's teeth pulverized the chalky tablet. He swallowed and cleared his throat. "What the hell. Arthur's in for a big surprise. That California blonde he intends to feature in his new campaign just signed an exclusive contract with my West Coast agency.

"Listen, you two start dinner. I'm going to run up to the drugstore and get some more tablets. Maybe the liquid, if Sylvie's cooking. Need anything? Okay. See you in a bit."

"Ahhh . . . look at all this!" Sylvia started tossing plastic-bagged vegetables on the counter. "Mushrooms, green peppers, an onion, celery, garlic. Oh . . . and here's a package of ground sirloin, cream, and"—she held up a bottle—"a hearty Burgundy." Noting Marlayna's forlorn expression, she hastily reached for two wineglasses. "Let's start with a glass for the cook."

After investigating the pantry, Sylvia returned with a large package of wide noodles, spices and another bottle of wine. "This should help pickle Paul's ulcer and numb your system into a good night's sleep." She pointed her companion toward the countertop range. "Put a pan of water on to boil and start browning the beef. I'd let you chop the veggies, but in your vacuous condition, giving you a knife is probably not a brilliant idea. Come to think of it . . . I'm not sure about the stove either."

"Enough already." Marlayna held her hands up in a gesture of surrender. "I'll stop thinking and start cooking." She aimed the faucet into the Dutch oven. "It's amazing how days later you can always find a better way to say what you did." She turned the large burner on high and reached for a copper-bottomed skillet that was suspended from the wooden ceiling rack. "Things would have worked out so much better if I had had the opportunity of an instant replay."

Sylvia stopped chopping and lifted her glass in a toasting gesture. "I'll drink to that, sweetie. Instant replay. If we all could live even one moment over again."

"Yeah." She broke up the sizzling meat with a wooden spoon, adjusting the heat so it wouldn't burn. "Just one moment. One silly little moment." Marlayna reached up and grabbed a shaker.

"Hey! You just dumped pepper into the boiling water!"

"Oh. I"—she sighed—"I could use an instant replay right now."

The doorbell sounded in the kitchen. "Put some fresh water on while I let Paulie in," Sylvia directed. "We can use two extra hands."

"I picked up some flowers. Thought they might help." Paul handed her a small bouquet. "How's she doing? Sylvie? Sylvie!" He waved his hand across the blonde's face.

She looked over his shoulder at the masculine figure whose cane was holding open the etched glass street door. "I have a hunch she's going to be doing better."

Turning, Paul followed the silent instructions of

Sylvia's jerking thumb. "Better? Maybe worse." His broad-shouldered denim-clad frame moved to block the door. "Noah Drake, right?"

"That's right." Noah's dark eyes inspected Paul's fighter stance and set expression. He offered his hand. "I'd like to thank you for all you've done for Mimi."

"I'd like to punch you for all you've put her through."

Sylvia stepped into the breach and accepted Noah's greeting. "Paul does a wonderful imitation of a lion, doesn't he?" She gave him a dazzling smile. "I trust you're here for a joyous reunion, because if you're not, we'll both punch you."

Noah blinked at her and nodded.

She exhaled a relieved sigh. "In that case, Marlayna's in the kitchen boiling pepper." Sylvia untied the small white apron that protected her white jumpsuit and tossed it at Noah. "Paulie, let's you and I adjourn to that Hungarian joint and play spin-the-paprika to see who gets to be maid of honor at their wedding."

"But . . . but . . . but . . ."

"You sound like a motorboat, doesn't he, Noah?" She gave the gray-haired modeling agent a shove into the hallway. "Come on, Paulie, this nice man has better things to do than listen to you make sound effects." Sylvia nodded. "The kitchen is straight through the white cafe doors." She hesitated a moment, then added, "Please, just ignore anything dumb she might say. A woman in love doesn't always enjoy common sense."

"Neither does a man," Noah returned with a grateful smile. A few minutes later, his trembling hand pushed open the louvered door. Marlayna had her back to him, her attention focused on various bubbling and boiling pots. Even when the door swung back, hinges squeaking, she didn't turn her head.

"I put salt in the water this time, Sylvie." Marlayna idly stirred the vegetable and beef mixture. "But I haven't stopped thinking about Noah. God, if I were him, I'd hop on a plane and come here just to strangle me!"

"Strangling wasn't at all what I had in mind."

The wooden spoon clattered to the floor, sending a shower of food over the counter and oven. She still didn't turn around. "You know this happened to me in the kitchen once before. I heard Noah's voice, but he wasn't really here."

Two arms wrapped around her waist and pulled her back against a very solid body. "I'm very real. And I'm here," his deep voice whispered into her ear. "Here for good. Unless you've changed your mind?"

A joyous cry caught in her throat; she turned and flung her arms around his neck. "Never." She blinked rapidly, trying to hold back tears. "I'm afraid you'll always be stuck with me. For better or worse——"

He tightened his embrace. "In sickness and in health——"

"For all eternity." She stroked back a lock of dark hair that had fallen across his forehead. "Noah . . . I'm . . . I'm so sorry for what I did and what I said. Can you ever forgive me?"

Laughter rumbled in his chest. "Forgive you? Love, I want to thank you." His eyes focused on her half-parted lips. "To kiss you." A hungry groan escaped him as his mouth formed a vital merger with hers.

She was breathless when he finally released her, her words coming in short gasps. "Oh, Noah, I was so afraid I'd never see you again."

"You're right about one thing." He gave her a crooked smile. "You won't be seeing the Noah Drake you left on Jorstadt Island again. He made it through the rain and found his self-respect." Noah reached around, turned off the burners and held out his hand. "Come on, let's go sit and talk."

He sat in the center of the white sofa and guided Marlayna onto his lap. "There's a lot I want to say to you. The first"—his knuckles caressed the hollow of her cheek—"is that I love you very much and for the same reasons I fell in love with you eight years ago. You are strong, capable, talented, intelligent, witty and beautiful, both inside and out. You are truly my better half."

She snuggled against his chest, her head comfortably ensconced in the curve of his shoulder, her right hand entwined with his left. "Those were the same words that precipitated our terrible fight. What made you decide that you can live with a woman who has those attributes?"

"Because you kept telling me I possessed those same attributes, but I wasn't smart enough to see it. I had to experience it." His forefinger lifted her chin. "Do you know how long it takes for a man with bionic knees and a cane to walk eight miles in the pouring rain?"

"How long?"

"Seven hours."

Marlayna winced. "Ouch."

"That's what I said while Perkins helped me into the whirlpool and kept pouring the brandy. Saturday morning I couldn't move. All the real muscles had tightened and the artificial ones refused to work."

"Oh . . . Noah . . . I'm so sorry."

He stilled her lips with a gentle finger. "Don't be. I

was extremely proud of myself. I made it without anyone's help." Noah shifted slightly. "I really shouldn't say that. You were my inspiration. At times I yelled, cursed, begged, pleaded and talked to you."

"What did you say?"

Noah took a deep breath. "I said, 'Mimi, I guess I forgot to mention the fact that I have yet to go out into the real world.' My Atlanta office was nothing more than a rehabilitation halfway house. You were rattling on and on about New York, and I had never left the safe womb of the island in two years except to have my therapy sessions.

"Perkins was my mother, caring and providing for me. The hospital and staff were old friends. And quite frankly I was scared. Scared to face people, scared to really start my career and scared that you would end up taking care of me.

"I didn't want that. I wanted to be the provider, the king of my castle, the ruler of the roost." He held up a peremptory palm. "Yes, I know, you don't have to say it. Mr. Macho. I never thought I was a male chauvinist. In fact, I always believed I was pretty damn liberated."

Marlayna was silent a moment. "What made the chauvinist reform?"

"Common sense. We were in exactly the same position before the accident. You had passed your exam and started in the medical lab at a big jump in salary while I still had my finals. Sure, I had received an offer to apprentice, but I was only able to say yes because of your job.

"And that was exactly what I was bitching about now. Your career was going to make it possible for me to finally have one. Instead of thanking you, I was berating you. Instead of being proud of your success, I was feeling inadequate about my own."

Noah's hands curved around her upper arms, straightening her up so he could look into her eyes. "Mimi, I am so very proud of you. You've done so much and come so far these past years, all on your own. You deserve every success and every happiness."

She leaned close against him, her lips a scant inch away from his. "You are my happiness. Having you back in my life makes me feel . . . complete. Whole. And very, very happy." Her kiss was sweet, her body pliant as it molded against his sinewy frame. A giggle escaped Marlayna. "What happened with Arthur and Gwen?"

"Mt. Saint Helen's outburst was a burp compared to theirs," Noah recounted. "I let Arthur expel all his lava and then let him have it. You were right about that, too. He enjoys playing the bully but backs down when confronted. Believe it or not, we ended up— friends. Or as close to friends as Arthur would let anyone be. I do know he respects me."

"Gwen?"

"Hell hath no fury like a woman scorned," came his rueful answer. "But for a scorned woman she was quickly soothed by that golf pro. Nothing like ardent devotion."

Marlayna's eyes narrowed. "I want some ardent devotion, too."

"Do you? Just what did you have in mind?"

Her tongue traced the outline of his lips before trespassing inside to find its mate. Her fingers released the buttons on his gray striped shirt so her hand could press into his heated flesh.

"I love it when you touch me," he groaned against her lips. "I love the feel of you against me." In one sweeping motion, he pulled her cotton top over her head and deftly removed her lace bra. "You are so beautiful."

Noah eased her backward onto the cushions, his mouth and hands never leaving her silken skin. His teeth and tongue coaxed her nipple into ripe awareness while he unsnapped her jeans so he could explore the wonders of her femininity.

She moaned softly, delighting in the rapturous sensations he was giving her. "Do I get a marriage proposal? I'll let you forgo the bended knees."

His head lifted from her breast, the love in his eyes more vivid than any words. "Will you do me the honor of becoming my wife?"

Marlayna cupped his handsome face between her hands. "I can't think of anything I'd rather be." Her lips returned a message that was filled with love and the promise of a wonderful future.

"Mimi, I'm home."

She smiled at him, held up her palm and finished her phone conversation. Before the receiver had fallen into place, she was wrapped in his arms. "I love hearing you say that when you walk in the door."

"Not bored yet? Even after three months?"

Her lingering kiss was her only answer. "I do have some good news, great news and wonderful news."

Noah eyed her curiously. "Start with the good."

"That was Perkins; he's saying good-bye to King Arthur and hello to the Drakes."

"Hey, that's terrific . . . but . . . we've already got Pearl."

"She goes with this place," Marlayna reminded him. "Our new house will be finished in another two months and we're going to be needing some help." Her fingers straightened the knot in his tan knit tie.

"That's my great news. Paul has a new contract for me."

"Will you be gone often?" His hands tightened into the curve of her slender waist.

"Nope. Just a few hours here and there, but it's very lucrative."

Noah frowned. "Sounds too sporadic to be lucrative. But Paul should know. What is it? Cosmetics?"

Marlayna shook her head. "Clothes." Blue gray eyes locked into brown. "Maternity clothes. That's my wonderful news."

"Oh, baby!" He surprised himself by lifting her off the floor.

She laughed. "That's exactly what the doctor said!"

"Uhh . . . shouldn't you be sitting down? Lying down?" Noah's words were as disjointed as his actions.

She captured his gesturing hand between hers and smiled. "Darling, that's exactly how I got in this wonderful condition!"

YOU'LL BE SWEPT AWAY WITH SILHOUETTE DESIRE

$1.75 each

1 ☐ James   5 ☐ Baker   8 ☐ Dee

2 ☐ Monet   6 ☐ Mallory   9 ☐ Simms

3 ☐ Clay   7 ☐ St. Claire   10 ☐ Smith

4 ☐ Carey

$1.95 each

11 ☐ James	29 ☐ Michelle	47 ☐ Michelle	65 ☐ Allison
12 ☐ Palmer	30 ☐ Lind	48 ☐ Powers	66 ☐ Langtry
13 ☐ Wallace	31 ☐ James	49 ☐ James	67 ☐ James
14 ☐ Valley	32 ☐ Clay	50 ☐ Palmer	68 ☐ Browning
15 ☐ Vernon	33 ☐ Powers	51 ☐ Lind	69 ☐ Carey
16 ☐ Major	34 ☐ Milan	52 ☐ Morgan	70 ☐ Victor
17 ☐ Simms	35 ☐ Major	53 ☐ Joyce	71 ☐ Joyce
18 ☐ Ross	36 ☐ Summers	54 ☐ Fulford	72 ☐ Hart
19 ☐ James	37 ☐ James	55 ☐ James	73 ☐ St. Clair
20 ☐ Allison	38 ☐ Douglass	56 ☐ Douglass	74 ☐ Douglass
21 ☐ Baker	39 ☐ Monet	57 ☐ Michelle	75 ☐ McKenna
22 ☐ Durant	40 ☐ Mallory	58 ☐ Mallory	76 ☐ Michelle
23 ☐ Sunshine	41 ☐ St. Claire	59 ☐ Powers	77 ☐ Lowell
24 ☐ Baxter	42 ☐ Stewart	60 ☐ Dennis	78 ☐ Barber
25 ☐ James	43 ☐ Simms	61 ☐ Simms	79 ☐ Simms
26 ☐ Palmer	44 ☐ West	62 ☐ Monet	80 ☐ Palmer
27 ☐ Conrad	45 ☐ Clay	63 ☐ Dee	81 ☐ Kennedy
28 ☐ Lovan	46 ☐ Chance	64 ☐ Milan	82 ☐ Clay

YOU'LL BE SWEPT AWAY WITH SILHOUETTE DESIRE

$1.95 each

83 ☐ Chance	97 ☐ James	111 ☐ Browning	125 ☐ Caimi
84 ☐ Powers	98 ☐ Joyce	112 ☐ Nicole	126 ☐ Carey
85 ☐ James	99 ☐ Major	113 ☐ Cresswell	127 ☐ James
86 ☐ Malek	100 ☐ Howard	114 ☐ Ross	128 ☐ Michelle
87 ☐ Michelle	101 ☐ Morgan	115 ☐ James	129 ☐ Bishop
88 ☐ Trevor	102 ☐ Palmer	116 ☐ Joyce	130 ☐ Blair
89 ☐ Ross	103 ☐ James	117 ☐ Powers	131 ☐ Larson
90 ☐ Roszel	104 ☐ Chase	118 ☐ Milan	132 ☐ McCoy
91 ☐ Browning	105 ☐ Blair	119 ☐ John	133 ☐ Monet
92 ☐ Carey	106 ☐ Michelle	120 ☐ Clay	134 ☐ McKenna
93 ☐ Berk	107 ☐ Chance	121 ☐ Browning	135 ☐ Charlton
94 ☐ Robbins	108 ☐ Gladstone	122 ☐ Trent	136 ☐ Martel
95 ☐ Summers	109 ☐ Simms	123 ☐ Paige	137 ☐ Ross
96 ☐ Milan	110 ☐ Palmer	124 ☐ St. George	138 ☐ Chase

SILHOUETTE DESIRE, Department SD/6
1230 Avenue of the Americas
New York, NY 10020

Please send me the books I have checked above. I am enclosing $_____
(please add 75¢ to cover postage and handling. NYS and NYC residents please
add appropriate sales tax). Send check or money order—no cash or C.O.D.'s
please. Allow six weeks for delivery.

NAME_____

ADDRESS_____

CITY_____ STATE/ZIP_____